73

Kissing Oscar Wilde
a novel

☙

by Jade Sylvan

Write Bloody Publishing
America's Independent Press

Austin, TX

WRITEBLOODY.COM

Sylvan, Jade.
1ˢᵗ edition.
ISBN: 978-1938912-32-0

Interior Layout by Lea C. Deschenes
Cover Design and Art by Lily Lin
Author Photo by Caleb Cole
Interior photos by Caleb Cole and Adélaïde Pornet
Proofread by Alex Kryger
Edited by Abigail Marshall and Derrick Brown
French translations by Lucie Monroe
Type set in Bergamo from www.theleagueofmoveabletype.com

Printed in Tennessee, USA

Write Bloody Publishing
Austin, TX
Support Independent Presses
writebloody.com

To contact the author, send an email to writebloody@gmail.com

MADE IN THE USA

KISSING OSCAR WILDE

Table of Contents

Photos

All beautiful things belong to the same age.

—Oscar Wilde

Précis
We'll Always Have Paris

*C*aleb and I met Adélaïde just before we made it to Paris. Adélaïde wore a Humphrey Bogart hat and cowboy boots and showed me and Caleb around Dijon, cobblestone and gargoyles dressed in dusky mist. Adélaïde loved Patti Smith and so did I and so did Caleb. Caleb and I had gone to see Patti Smith sing in Providence years before because I was a poet and Caleb was a photographer and we had always joked that I was Patti Smith and he was Robert Mapplethorpe. When I read Patti Smith's book, *Just Kids*, I cried and texted Caleb from Tucson to make sure he knew that I loved him. I asked Adélaïde if she had read *Just Kids*, but she hadn't because it was too hard to find in French.

Adélaïde was a poet and an actor. Later, on the internet, I saw a piece a French news station had done about poetry and performance. Adélaïde talked to the camera about self-expression, and they wrote under her name, *poetesse Dijoinaise*.

She blew her nose constantly.

She gave me a paper notebook.

I'm writing in it right now.

It's 2012. I don't believe in gender, I'm perpetually in love with around fifteen separate people at any given time, and I haven't written in a paper notebook for four years. I spend too much time on the internet looking at faces of people I used to know. I blow my nose constantly. I think sometimes how we're all separate and all lonely in our skins surrounded by empty space, and how everyone wants to break their skins and become soup with everyone else and that's why "the internet," and then I don't feel so bad about all the time I spend on it.

When Adélaïde came to meet me in Paris, I gave her a copy of a poem I had written for a man named Louis. The poem was about Paris and Arthur Rimbaud and a man I was in love with a long time before I was in love with Louis. Louis had dark, wild hair and loved Arthur Rimbaud. I was in love with Louis because his name was Leaf and mine was Sylvan and when we met he said, *I could be a Leaf in your forest*, and I said, *This looks like the start of a beautiful friendship* because *Casablanca* was my favorite movie, and then forever afterward, he called me Rick and I called him Louis. We talked about loving Arthur Rimbaud. I went to Paris, in part, because I was hoping to impress Louis, who loved Paris, or at least loved a woman (who was not me) who loved Paris.

When I met Adélaïde, I said, *This looks like the start of a beautiful friendship,* because Adélaïde was as beautiful as Louis. She said *Casablanca* was her favorite movie. She'd seen it in French on the internet.

Louis is not on the internet because he believes in paper love. I see Adélaïde on the internet. I carry the notebook she gave me everywhere.

I get the feeling sometimes that these people I love are all the same person. This is chauvinistic, I know.

The word "chauvinism" comes from Napoleon's soldier Nicholas Chauvin, who blindly loved the Empire long after it fell. The word "romance" originally referred to the vernacular language of France. I wouldn't know any of this without the internet.

I wouldn't be able to see the news story about Adélaïde without the internet. I would know almost nothing about her.

I love Caleb when we take pictures or talk about taking pictures. In real life, he's neurotic and difficult to touch.

I love Louis when I write six evenly-measured, six-lined stanzas about him. In real life, his slouch annoys me and he smokes too much.

I don't know if I love these people or if I just love to write about them.

Or maybe I just love Paris.

I don't know if I really know Paris. It's been written about too many times.

But I love Patti Smith.

Patti Smith loved Arthur Rimbaud. In *Just Kids*, she writes about flying to Paris just to write about him. Adélaïde is back in Dijon now. When I got back to the States, I bought her a copy of *Just Kids* in French on the internet. She says she carries the book, and the poem I gave her, everywhere.

I get the feeling sometimes that we are, all of us, the same person, across time and space, loving ourselves from afar, star-crossed and lonely.

Maybe that part of us that's the same in everyone is a moth, drawn to the light of computer screens and cities.

Maybe that part of us is a messenger, sending ourselves desperate love notes inked on rustic paper, flawed and organic, unreadable in the dark.

Maybe that's why we always go looking for ourselves in the cities with the most light.

Chapter One
Graves

I spent a good portion of my late teens and early twenties making pilgrimages to my favorite authors' graves. By the time I officially met Caleb, I had already started to gather an impromptu mental catalogue of the physical tokens of these mass-conceptions. In Oxford, Mississippi, admirers leave William Faulkner cigarettes and bourbon. Ralph Waldo Emerson's grave is piled with pinecones. Rainer Maria Rilke is buried in a tiny churchyard at the very top of a tall, goat-dotted hill in the Swiss Alps, where panting young poets ascend to leave single, intentional roses. My favorite was Oscar Wilde, who lies in a relatively serene, tree-lined corner of Paris's labyrinthine celebrity cemetery, Père Lachaise. In the 1990s, fans started leaving lipstick kisses on the large rectangular stone sculpture that serves as his grave marker and headstone. The brighter the color, the better. There were hundreds of them. Hundreds on hundreds. Sometimes when everything was dark and I felt abandoned by everyone and couldn't stop thinking about lonely, diabetic women sitting in front of their televisions feeding on corn syrup and Paxil and nuggets made from mutant, drugged-up chickens who lived their whole lives force-fed in tiny cages, I would shut my eyes and picture those kisses, all red and pink against the grey, and a thumbprint-sized place in my chest would open to a warm, peaceful glow. If that many people could love the idea of this person, who died an outcast, so much so that they were independently and collectively moved to kiss the very symbol of death, then there was hope for everyone who had ever been shamed or excluded or ridiculed. There was even hope for me.

Chapter Two
Memento

*B*efore the pan-romantic exploits, the buzzing poetry bars, and the foggy draw of Paris, I grew up stagnant and strange in Indianapolis, Indiana. Nothing about me seemed to make sense in/to my surroundings. Kids called me a "freak" at school for reasons I never understood. To my conservative parents, I was confusingly artistic at the best of times and embarrassingly perverse at the worst. I felt placeless, so books became my home and their authors and characters became my closest friends for years until I went to college in Bloomington and found/ed a small group of queer artists, including[1] Caleb.

After I graduated, I knew I had to leave the Midwest. I decided on Boston for three reasons: one, Indiana was no place to be a writer, and Boston's literary scene seemed the closest to the 1920s Parisian Lost Generation or the 1950s San Francisco Beat world that I could imagine at the end of 2006; two, *The Sound and the Fury* was my favorite book at the time, and I thought Quentin's chapter was the most beautiful

---

1. Caleb and I actually met each other at least once before college, though he says he doesn't remember it. See the chapter: "An Ideal Husband."

thing ever written in English, and Quentin was at Harvard[2] when, in 20-year-old Rimbaud-esque mania, he broke his pocket watch to escape time and walked into the Charles River to drown; three, Caleb was moving to Boston for photography school.

My last few months in Bloomington, I would walk over to Caleb's house in the cruel heat of southern Indiana's August after teaching poetry to kids. It was the summer after I graduated college and the summer after his mother died. His forearms had two new tattoos in his mother's handwriting that were two of her favorite Latin phrases[3]. One said, *memento mori*, and the other said, *carpe diem*.

We would climb down the rocky bank of the stream by his house to take pictures under the graffitied bridge and talk about love, death, social constructs, and most of all, art. We talked about moving away from the utterly unbearable, all-pervading flatness of Indiana, its fields of corn and soybeans interrupted by dismal strip malls and monstrous chain restaurants. We talked about going to some city, some *real* city, and becoming a photographer and a writer, respectively, and how one day, when we were old (meaning like 40) and successful and ready to sell out, we would get some grants or whatever and use the money to travel around the world to different famous people's graves, and he would take pictures and I would write some bullshit something for each picture about what the items people leave there mean about what the person—or the idea of the person—meant to people. Then we would use all the money we would make to ensure we would never have to work at regular jobs again. Maybe we'd buy a warehouse or a farm that came with its own electricity and goats. Then we'd sprawl across hours and days shooting and writing and collage-ing and creating other brand-new modes of expression that we were sure it

---

2. I had no idea that later Louis and I would go, late one night, to the Harvard footbridge and find three tiny portraits of Quentin glued to the stone rail by an anonymous art student. We'd sit on the rail for some time looking at the moon reflect down the black river and tell each other about our respective experiences in Psych Wards.

3. "Favorite Latin phrases" is a thing some Catholics have.

would one day be our responsibility to invent, because we knew we couldn't spend half our waking lives at sallow nine-to-fives. We vowed we would never. That would be worse than death.

Chapter Three
Halloween 2011, Boston

*S*o, because I'd just been fired from a job I never wanted, and because I'd just come to the realization that everyone in America from baristas to CEOs, from groundskeepers to lawyers, is one bum-stroke away from total material upheaval and all its subsequent blows to the Self, and that everyone, no matter how much money they make, is always walking around quietly quelling the hum of the belief that they will die alone and penniless in some lukewarm, miasmic gutter in an unfamiliar city, and because I'd woken up again sweating bourbon into unwashed sheets in my ten-foot by ten-foot occupation in a house rented to me dirt-cheap by an entrepreneurial acquaintance out of pity/patronage after driving back to Boston ill-advisedly from Ralph's Rock Diner in Worcester, where poetry happens on Mondays and where, this Monday, uncostumed on Halloween for the first time in my life, I called Louis from the toilet and told him about my befiring and about my general failure as an adult and as an organism and my sudden stomachache and desire to die (because I'd always found calling those you wished would love you at the nadir of performative despondency produced a result, even if I'd never examined those results' favorableness) before getting onstage beneath a menagerie of taxidermied, ungulate faces and reading a poem that changed the air in the room, made the young tatted-up Straight Edgers and the scotch-pickled English Leather Fogies halt their chitchat and stare, literally stare at me with jaws agape, that made my buddy, Alex, take my arm oracularly and say, after two beers, *You know that poem is important, right?* and, after four beers, grab my shoulders and kiss me full on the mouth, and since Dareka, the French poet, had been assuring me that if I came to France in January I could count on bookings at all of the poetry venues and safe sofas to sleep on and all the pains au chocolat I could eat, and since even though it wasn't a real job, or even a character with a place-card in the societyscape of the 21st century, I had never seen myself as or wanted to be anything other than a poet, I thought, *fuck it*, took 750 of my last $1500, and bought myself a ticket.

Chapter Four
The Poem I Read at Ralph's Rock Diner in Worcester, Massachusetts

On Breathing

When you learn that most of what you've read and studied for in school
is a crude approximation or shrewd merchandizing tool,

and your lungs will one day shrivel, and your heart will fizzle out
when tricks of science peter and religion's sick with doubt,

and your rapist's hands weren't dirty, and forgiveness won't clean deeds,
and just cause something's dirty doesn't mean it seeds disease,

and your safety net's dispassion on this centripetal whirlwind,
and without the lights and makeup movie stars look like your girlfriend,

and your doctor's a mechanic, and your therapist's a nut,
and your head and heart betray you till you only trust your gut,

and Hitler was a vegan, and an artist, and a Jew,
and Hussein was not a devil, and your father's half of you,

it can be hard to keep on going, but you do.

When knees wake stiff, reminding you that death's your only birthright,
and there seems to be some script you lost to move across the earth right,

and soil swallows all your clothes, books, houses, clocks, and letters,
and credit scores and income are the first things in the shredder,

and your synapses are labyrinths that coax desirous heat,
and beneath their skins your enemies, like you, are only meat,

and the pattern of his birthmarks and the odd bend of his hand
are death when you recall them and Inferno when you can't,

and the upright slouch in alleyways while Rupert Murdoch thrives,
and money is a symbol, and your children won't survive,

and vodka seems to work as well as any cheerful pill,
and college girls and soldiers look so young, and younger still,

it can be hard to keep on moving, but you will.

When masturbation's better than most lovers' hunger pangs,
and love produces chemicals, like chocolate and teen angst,

and you only feel by bleeding, and Top Tens have made love cheesy,
and all your pain's cliché, but that still doesn't make it easy,

and once you struck a song while wrestling with an old piano
and played it to an empty hall and hummed the sad soprano,

and the moon will never care for you, the sun will make you blind,
and there're rooms locked in your body even you will never find,

and her back is pressed against your chest, her scapula are wings,
and sex is high and sacred, just like every other thing,

and your belly's slightly fat and gapped with stretch marks where it grew,
and you know you'll never meet someone who'll love you more than you,

and you wake up in some room alone, the sunlight cold as flan,
your skin saran against the dawn, the door, a businessman,

it can be hard keep on breathing, but you can.

Chapter Five
Une Saison en Enfer

$\mathcal{I}$ started to work with the French poet Dareka to plan my tour almost immediately after buying my ticket to Paris. He had connections all over Europe, and gigs came through surprisingly easily. Within weeks, I had shows lined up in Barcelona, Amsterdam, Dijon, and Reims. The tour would end with several days in Paris.

As the dates fell into place, I started to feel as though it were possible that I wasn't completely delusional after all, and, maybe, this really was what I was supposed to be doing with my life. I was a poet, wasn't I? Poets are obsessed with Paris, aren't they? The fact that Louis was also obsessed with Paris admittedly intensified the City of Light's immediate allure.

I met Louis three days before the end of 2010. I first ran up to him, grabbed his arm, and said *You're going to be my friend*, because he'd just gone onstage, black shock-tangle of hair and black button-up against ghost-white skin, and read a rollicking suicide-watch bus ride manifesto in a quagmire of self-conscious post-post-modern reflections on college life, a flicker-eyed oration causing every throat and jaw in the whole urine-soaked basement of the Cantab Lounge to constrict and gape with since-outmoded early-20th century ecstasies. As he finished a page he'd fling it above him, each leaf flashing in the stagelights before floating to the floor, until finally he threw up his hands and walked straight into the crowd and directly to the bar. The audience stood, stomped, and cheered. Now *that* was a poet. I rose and followed him through the break in the bodies.

When I declared we would be friends, he suggested we smoke. I didn't smoke but made exceptions for shared moments with the exceptionally talented, intelligent and/or beautiful. I followed him outside and took one of his Winstons. I was wearing the dashing grey pea coat I'd bought in Germany four years earlier, but it wasn't warm enough for Boston's December and I was shivering. I asked him who his favorite poets were, and he said Allen Ginsberg and Arthur Rimbaud. I told him that the Halloween before, I performed an abridged version of *A Season in Hell* as Arthur Rimbaud[4] in the Dead Poets Show at the Cantab Lounge. I asked what Louis did when he wasn't cracking open dank poetry basements in Cambridge. He was a playwright, just graduated from Harvard. He was currently living part-time with an introverted Francophile polyamorous girlfriend and part-time as a caretaker for a cantankerous nonagenarian, who every evening told him the same tragic story concerning the death of Vaudeville.

Katabasis, he said. *That's the word that describes my current situation.*

I didn't know it.

It's descent. It's Oscar Wilde dying an outcast in the gutter as his fop friends clink champagne glasses in a restaurant across the street.

As he talked, I smoked. I taught myself how to smoke holding the cigarette between my thumb and first two fingers like a joint, because that's how Bob Dylan smoked in *Don't Look Back*. I remembered

---

4. Caleb helped me bind my chest with a back brace and an ace bandage and showed me how to strengthen my jaw with a line of brown eye shadow under my chin and speak from my chest voice— though Rimbaud was around 16 at the time and so probably sounded a lot like my normal speaking voice.

reading in *Just Kids* how Patti Smith used to try to move like Bob Dylan moved in *Don't Look Back* when she walked away from someone she was trying to impress. I wasn't sure if I was imitating Bob Dylan, or Patti Smith imitating Bob Dylan, or Patti Smith imitating Bob Dylan imitating Arthur Rimbaud.

As soon as he finished his first cigarette, Louis lit another. His eyes sparked when he smiled. He reminded me of someone, but I couldn't quite pinpoint who it was. I could, however, feel my lungs turning blacker with every breath. Then I remembered reading a quote from Patti Smith in the 1990s about herself as a young woman. *I had devoted so much of my girlish daydreams to Rimbaud,* she said. *Rimbaud was like my boyfriend.*

I grounded out my cigarette with the heel of my cowboy boot and turned to go back downstairs. I couldn't manage *Don't Look Back.* My left leg is oddly assembled and makes me limp even when I try to be impressive, even when I try my hardest just to walk away.

Chapter Six
An Epically-Abridged Catalogue of the Author's Major Romances, Revealing the Young Midwestern Author's Odyssey Through Fluid Sexuality

Marissa

A conflation of a series of close female friends of the teenaged author's who she was totally attracted to and who, in retrospect, were totally attracted to her, but who she never did anything with other than write them cute, rhyming poems, drive them to *The Taming of the Shrew* rehearsal or Rocky Horror or Bible Study, and sometimes share the same bed with them during sleepovers and let her pinky finger slip over their pinky finger or her thigh rest into their thigh.

Will

The author's first "relationship." Dated the author for six months, from author's age 18 to just past 19. A tech geek who enjoyed gaming

LANs and performing cunnilingus and who, excitingly to the author's parents, had a penis and a future. During a defining conversation at Mother Bear's Pizza which eventually led to their breakup, he told the author that aspiring to be a poet was essentially *aspiring to be a crack whore on the street,* which did not set her down her current life-path but certainly hardened her resolve. At the current time of writing, he is an investment banker on Wall Street. He invited the author to his wedding in 2011, but she was busy.

Thade

Practically married to the author for five years, from author's age 19-24. A classical composer and poet. Loved Charles Baudelaire, Jean Cocteau, Rainer Maria Rilke, John Cage, the Beat Generation, etc. Accompanied the author on her first trip to Europe in 2006 and shared her kiss on Oscar Wilde's tomb. All of the author's friends and family thought he was gay, but his womanishness with the author's mannishness worked. The author was also allowed to make out with girls during this romance, which was a big plus for the author. He and the author thought they were soulmates. They would've gotten tattoos of the two face-halves from *Hedwig and the Angry Inch* if he hadn't been too much of a wuss to get tattooed.

Leigh

A conflation of four to five inconsiderately-pretty, pixyish young women with Borderline Personality Disorder with whom the author would attend Tori Amos concerts, make out in movie theaters as she wiped away their tears during screenings of *The Hours,* and exchange cunnilingus after hits of nitrous oxide while their boyfriends discussed critical theory in the next room.

Dawn

The reason the author started getting tattooed. A gamine, freckled, menthol-smoking high-school dropout with green eyes that no-joke sparkled, expansive dreams, and an even more expansive theory of her global importance. Her arms were covered in fairy tattoos that represented the four elements and scars from years working the hot ovens in pizza kitchens. She was one of those Leos who's really into being a Leo. She was always falling out, getting fired, and raging against various establishments. This romance led the author to lose a great deal of sleep and weight.

Owen

A conflation of several brilliant, sensitive, romantically-unavailable males with whom the author shared artistically collaborative relationships with obvious romantic overtones. All of these men smoked Winstons. The invariable zenith of each of these relationships was a night spent sharing past-relationship fucked-upness, splitting an entire bottle of bourbon, and listening to Jeff Buckley's album, *Grace*, from start to finish lying on separate sofas in the dark.

Luke

An average man of average intelligence with average drinking and anger-management problems. He wrote average poetry and held down average day jobs. All of the author's friends hated him, and she knew it but almost loved that they hated him. For the first time since dating Will, the author could imagine filling a sitcom-suitable, hetero-normative female role, complete with drunken verbal abuse, emotional neglect, and repeated devaluation of all of the author's endeavors. The fact that the author associates these characteristics with the heteronormative female role, the author admits, says a lot about her relationship to heteronormative culture.

Chapter Seven
Abstinence

*L*ouis and I never actually slept together, even though we met at the height of the period in my life I refer to as my "sexual terrorist" phase. Luke and I had officially broken up in the fall of 2010 after he downed eight shots of Jack Daniel's during one of my shows, jumped onstage during the middle of a skit, and announced, from his chest voice, that I was "an ungrateful bitch." After a few weeks of female-empowerment beach trips, long back-porch heart-to-hearts that ended with me crashing wine-drunk on friends' couches, countless reassurances from Caleb, and lots of yoga, I decided, at 28, it was time to figure out how to be a proper slut.

I spent six months sleeping with everyone—friends of friends on pull-out couches after dinner parties, poetry groupies at out-of-town shows. I found my way into boudoir-lit burlesque cast parties and glitter-strewn pan-gender sex clubs. Yes, I made poems out of all of it. Sometimes I told the people in the poems and sometimes I didn't. Once I carried a case of scabies from Owen's bed[5] to the bed of his

---

5. This was the only Owen I ever actually slept with.

platonic roommate, Leigh[6]. Neither one of them thought the situation was as funny as I did[7]. That became a poem too. I told one of them.

I meant to be mindful of everyone's feelings. A couple of times, however, I'd get a text from someone I'd slept with asking me to come with them when they got their Lasik surgery, or to meet their sister in from Baltimore, and I finally knew how guys feel when they accidentally hurt girls out of sheer ignorant self-absorption. The way I knew when I'd fucked up was my stomach would hurt.

A drinking buddy of mine said once that sex without an emotional connection is masturbation with a friend. I was amazed at how easily I acted out the physical. I was aware of how every one of my actions was received, even through an orgasm. I watched myself make every scratch, every bite and moan. This must be enlightenment, I'd tell myself: bright and shiny bodily sex without the dark egoic weight of romance.

While all this was happening, Louis and I began our weird, sexless romance. The day after we met, he emailed me the poem I first saw him read, and I sent him my poem, "Plates." He wrote back on New Year's Eve:

> *Dear Rick,*
>
> *Something like a year or two ago in one of my rants about the general guarded dross of academic+confessional poetry, I said to one of my friends that I had just heard some girl at the Cantab read something about dirty dishes and Tibetan burial that was so much better than all that shit, and was not so much "the next thing," but was in fact just, "the thing"; that she was better than everything I'd heard at any readings*

---

6. This is slightly poeticized. Technically, Leigh and I were in *my* bed

7. In fact, Leigh kind of lost it for a while and started burning her clothes and scrubbing her skin until it bled. I definitely felt bad about that.

at Harvard or in any spoken word society; and that this girl had some seriously hot blood that gave me hope. I thought that it might have been you, but now I know it obviously is and that it all makes sense now. So thank you. I'll write back more in full later and send you another.

See you in the decade fresh.

Louis

We went on a couple of unspoken pseudo-dates, but after this email, his relationship with his girlfriend deteriorated and he moved back to his parents' house in Ann Arbor. We continued to email poems back and forth. We called each other "friend" and managed to shackle the word with innuendo.

Late in the spring of 2011, he moved to Connecticut to work at a theatre in New Haven. He would call me whenever he came through town, and no matter how tired I was, we would stay up late-late, talking and laughing and looking over each other's poetry. When were in the same room, everything became funny—sentence structure and words and breathing and being bodies—all of it just absurd.

One night at the beginning of the summer, we processed down to Jamaica Pond post-house show with a small group of poets. When we reached the black water, shrouded by trees from the urban commercial street, some of us began to peel off our clothes. We waded into the water, one by one, gorgeous, sinking silhouettes between different shades of dark—pond, trees, sky. When I was in up to my ribs, I lay down and floated. It was the middle of the city but I could only see stars. I was everything, and everything was silent and weightless.

Louis stayed clothed on the bank with the two body-shy college girls. He told me later it was because he had jock-itch, not because he was not fun-loving and star-gazing.

Louis and I only ever kissed once, smoking his Winstons outside Redbones Barbeque late in September. I told him I was tired of struggling and being poor and how I'd just sold out and taken a real job. He told me I was a poet, that I couldn't help but be a poet, and that someone else can do the PR for the biggest yoga studio in Cambridge. It was clear at that moment that Louis should not be another Owen, and this was so evidently that turning point in every romantic movie when the only correct action was to kiss this man. I leaned over and kissed him, and it ruined our friendship. That was when I decided I didn't know a thing about romance.

I read an article in *The New Yorker* that said we Americans don't know how to deal with love that isn't either sexual or familial. My polyamorous friends gave me books that said attraction is attraction, that it's just situational, imposed limits that keep us, sometimes, from fucking those with whom we share push/pull eye-contact or Beatrice/Bene-diction. I read a lot that fall.

Just before I left, I read an article about how they cleaned all the kisses off Oscar Wilde's grave. It made my stomach hurt the way it hurt when I was nine and I learned about global warming and the atomic bomb[8]. I texted Louis about it from some bar with an anachronistic, overwrought tone of despair. He responded with a deeply poetic blow-off. That night I wrote a poem called "Kissing Oscar Wilde."

When I told Caleb about the kisses and the grave, we were in his living room about to watch a Woody Allen movie about Paris. We were eating sea salt brownies. I think I must have been almost crying, or else my voice must have sounded dead. Caleb has always wanted to make things better for me. He said immediately that he would come meet me in Paris while I was on tour and that we could go back to Oscar Wilde's grave and replace my kiss, or do something else in response—a statement, a happening—and he would take pictures.

---

8. I was nine when I started to write poetry.

I also read how some unmarried born-again Christians become abstinent when they convert—a second virginity, they call it. I thought that maybe I'd learned how to love all wrong and that maybe if I recreated the circumstances of my adolescence, I could reprogram that part of my brain. When I arrived in Paris, I'd been abstinent for six months.

In case you were wondering, Caleb and I have never kissed.

Chapter Eight
The Poem I Wrote for Louis
and Would Later Give to Adélaïde

Kissing Oscar Wilde

Two beers in I text you about Oscar Wilde and how I left my kiss
on his tomb at Père Lachaise when I was young like Rimbaud
and how I'd just read how They'd washed off all the lipstick,
all those loving kisses, because the grease was eroding the work
of modernist sculptor Jacob Epstein, and how They'd erected
a glass barrier to protect the stone angel from irreparable damage.

I tell you about my ex-boyfriend and how we slathered our lips a
shimmering mauve shade (all the proceeds went to fight AIDS),
found a naked corner and planted our vandal worship, giggling
naive ecstasies, took a picture with our camera (this was before
phones were cameras), and kissed under the silver sky among the dead
and the French (I still miss him sometimes—I don't tell you that).

Even Wilde's own grandson Merlin said, about the glass, *Maybe one
day we can take it down when the memory of kissing Oscar is gone.*
How many times can They take his love away from him? I ask you

(like you know). Haven't They learned yet that love is never clean?
You say sometimes the effort to preserve something is what renders it
truly dead, and how They're idiots and are always ruining things like this.

When I was young I followed the proud poetic tradition of quarreling
loudly in the inebriate streets of the Left Bank. Our kisses broke
us down to elements and stained us with grease, sloppy and earnest.
I tell you about lipstick on stone, how when the pigments fade the
stains spread to ovals and they don't even look like mouths anymore.
You say he will be mourned by outcasts, and outcasts always mourn.

I don't tell you how I wish you'd seen me when I was skinny
and angry, smoking cigarettes, taking shots, writing important,
terrible poetry in leather notebooks, hungry for hunger itself,
kissing in French graveyards, still romantic enough to be cynical.
Rimbaud'd be dead by now. Morrison, too. I worry I've outlived
the romantics. Thousands of kisses have worn me down.

I'm in a bar full of acquaintances and I text you about Oscar Wilde
because no one here is getting out alive, and we're both writers, so
we know what not to say—how we've ruined everything and hell is
seasonal (tourists are kissing trees), how the cleansing of the oldest stains
leaves us covered in glass till the memory of kissing is gone, and how
there's something underneath all this and we dare not speak its name.

Chapter Nine
Gare de Lyon

*N*ear the end of 2006, I'd taken four months to chase history and couch-surf through the old cobblestone continent. I feared the trip might just be a played-out American, white-kid postponement of adulthood—a last grasp at adolescence before moving to Boston and scrounging to afford shared housing in the rat-colonized part of town. I figured, though, that Patti Smith did it when she was young, and if it was good enough for twenty-four-year-old Patti Smith, it was good enough for twenty-four-year-old Jeni Schaibley[9]. Plus, I wanted to be a poet.

Whatever my motivations, I placed my barely-adult body in lamp-lit Dublin pubs and stained-glass-lit Barcelona Cathedrals and tiny, candle-lit Parisian cafés, where I scrawled free verse rants and iambic villanelles detailing the import of it all in sticker-covered Moleskines and Mead Composition Notebooks, dragging Thade along with me even though our relationship had already started to fall apart.

Near the beginning of 2012, Julian and I carried our bags up to the train station. Julian was a poet I knew from the Boston scene a few

---

9. My name at the time.

years earlier who had moved to New York City to woo some guy and to "make it" as a poet, had since moved *out* of New York City when neither the guy nor the "making it" aligned with his expectations, and was now on an indefinite world tour which happened to coincide with my European tour for about a week and a half. When we realized this coincidence, we decided to combine forces and tour together.

Julian was very blond, very pretty, and, when he chose to be, extremely charming. He was currently dragging my suitcase on its rollers in addition to hoisting two heavy bags of his own. He was doing this partly because dragging things was hard on my bad left leg and partly because he was trying to make amends after losing his temper and shouting[10] at me in the train station in Amsterdam, which he did because he'd had a lousy show the night before involving some drunk old Dutch townie heckling anti-gay slurs while he was onstage. He'd apologized and I'd accepted, but we still weren't really talking.

I had recently cut my hair from a shoulder-length Patti Smith-inspired shag to a short Dylan-esque helmet of curls. I wore a gold, suede knee-length trench I'd found at an Indiana thrift store when I was fourteen, and Julian wore a brown and cream houndstooth he'd bought in Amsterdam two days before. Ours were the only coats that weren't black.

There was a goofy chain restaurant called "Indiana" across from Gare de Lyon. I remembered it. I'd stood in this exact spot five years earlier, when Thade and I had met my friend Orestis just as we got in to town from Germany. All three of us were from Indiana[11]. Next to the restaurant, there was a small bakery where we'd grabbed

---

10. Julian was convinced for most of the tour that he was cursed, as in, literally, and that everything was going right for me and wrong for him. When an automatic door closed on his suitcase, he'd tried to yank it free, which wound up twisting his wrist when the doors finally released. *This always happens!* he screamed at me, throwing his suitcase so it spun across the smooth floor of the train station. *I'm fucking sick of it, Jade! This always happens to me because of my fucking curse! I'm fucking done!*

11. In fact, Orestis would be my brother's best man the following spring.

strawberry tartes before heading back to Orestis's place in the 14th Arrondissement. I expected the landmarks to be the same—Tour Eiffel, Notre-Dame, Louvre—but this was incidental constancy. My idiot feelings were mildly hurt that Paris could and would go on, business as usual, unsympathetic to any individual humans who happened to come and go.

The leather soles of my cowboy boots slipped and slid on the smooth tile floors of the station. I bought them because Patti Smith wore cowboy boots when Caleb and I saw her in Providence and because the high arches were good for my bad knee. They were the only shoes I brought to France.

When we finally found Caleb, he was huddled on a bench, wearing a black coat and a black hat, surrounded by three black bags. His pale face[12] seemed to glow white.

In my head I'd pictured running up and giving him a giant hug for flying across the Atlantic to hang out with me on tour, but he was buried awkwardly in his baggage and had dark circles under his eyes.

Hey, I said.

And he said, *Hey.*

How are you?

I couldn't sleep on the plane at all and I came straight here from the airport. I've been here for five hours. I'm okay.

Oh my god, they have places you can lock your bag up and go walk around. I told you that in my email, I thought.

I know. It's fine. I didn't want to risk leaving my stuff. Or getting lost. Or something else happening. I'd rather just stay here and make sure I'm where I need to be.

Okay. Well, I'm glad you're here. Give me a hug.

---

12. The art critic oligarchy had decided in 2010 to take every opportunity to describe him as *moon faced*, which made me laugh every time.

Okay.

He stood up with his giant black camera bag over his shoulder and I hugged him and he hugged back. It was, like all Caleb hugs, slightly stiff and uncomfortable. Caleb was not a physically affectionate person. It was two years into our friendship before we could touch[13] this much.

This is Julian. Julian, this is Caleb.

They shook hands, and we waited for our track to be announced on the big board in the center of the station. I repeatedly looked at my phone attempting to check my email and Facebook messages, forgetting that my 3G didn't work in Europe. Finally, I just stood with the others in silence. It had been years since my brain had been forced to exist without constant internet access. It felt spacious. It felt like being a teenager.

When *Dijon 13:10—voie 8* lit up, we loaded up and dragged our bags to the platform. We looked at our tickets. Julian and I were seated together in car 26, and Caleb was in car 32.

Julian said, *Here, you two want to catch up, and I want to do some work anyway. Why don't we switch tickets?*

Caleb and I said okay.

We puzzle-pieced our bags into the already overfull luggage racks. A minute after we settled into our seats, the train started up, and I watched the city begin to move steadily behind us.

I'd been here before, only this time it was Caleb, not Thade, sitting next to me. Now, I had new scars and tattoos and memories. Returning

---

13. I got absurdly drunk at my brother's wedding, made out with Orestis, and then passed out in my bridesmaid dress on top of the comforter in my hotel room. Caleb found me there, face pressed into an allergy-inducing feather pillow, and called down to the front desk to bring me something hypoallergenic, which he then placed beneath my makeup-smeared and likely drooling head. In the morning, he said he was sorry he didn't put me in my pajamas, but even though he'd seen me naked dozens of times, he wasn't sure if our friendship was at the place where it was okay for him to undress and then redress my unconscious body. In retrospect, I appreciate his respect for my consent. At the time, I was hurt that he didn't think he had it.

someplace you've been before is not the same as going somewhere for the first time. There should really be a separate verb for it.

My normally severe allergies had been exacerbated by the dairy- and wheat-heavy European diet, and I started to tear up a napkin in which to blow my nose. Caleb was used to me blowing my nose all the time in public, and he didn't even look as I blew loudly, turned the makeshift tissue over, and blew again. He pulled his hat down over his eyes, folded his arms, and went to sleep. I tucked a snotty wad of paper into my pocket and kept my eyes open, trying to notice every inch of stone and as it passed, let it go.

I've never been to Paris in the summer. I only know it in monochrome—silver buildings, silver river, silver statues, silver sky. No one wears color. It almost looks like a black and white film.

Chapter Ten
An Ideal Husband

The first time I saw Caleb I was dressed as a boy. Caleb was a girl then, and her name was Carrie. I was sixteen, so she must have been seventeen. I had a haircut that my mom called "pixy" and my Drama Club friends called "butch." I was wearing my brother's carpenter jeans and polo shirt and my own Doc Marten boots. I'd smashed down my C-cup breasts with a sports bra and kept slouching to try to disguise them as pecks.

Marissa and I were in the theater department of one of Indianapolis's Catholic high schools, Cathedral, which was not our high school. We were waiting backstage for her friend Mary to finish a tech rehearsal. When she finally came back to meet us, Carrie was with her. Mary was about five-two and athletic-looking, with deep olive skin and *My So-Called Life* bottle-burgundy hair. She wore a black tank top with bright green bra straps showing. She had a real nose ring. Carrie was just as short, with pale skin and white-red hair. She was dressed more like I was, except she wasn't trying to hide her breasts, and they were bigger than mine anyway. I would've called Carrie's haircut "butch" and Mary's haircut "pixy." Mary talked a lot, but Carrie hardly said two words. I've told Caleb about this encounter several times but he doesn't remember it.

The next week at school Marissa told me Mary thought I was cute. She'd asked Marissa to pass along her phone number. I left the torn piece of green-inked paper on my dresser for a month before I finally threw it away. Then I started to wear platform sandals and grow out my hair.

Three years later, during my freshman year in college, I saw Carrie perform at a drag show in the lobby of my dorm. I remembered her pale skin and white-red hair from the Cathedral theater. Carrie's drag name was Caleb King. Later, when Carrie Colvard became Caleb Cole, he changed his drag name to Owen[14] King.

I saw Caleb again at a friend's birthday party late in the summer before I turned twenty-three. I was staying in Bloomington an extra year after I graduated, working at a women's shelter, going to therapy for Depression and Obsessive Compulsive Disorder, trying to write a novel, and waiting for Thade to finish his final year of school. Caleb had a faux-hawk and sideburns and was wearing a plain red t-shirt. I was in a slightly hipsterfied stage of femme-ness, with short, dyed-black hair, a black lace tank top, and high heels.

I remembered Caleb from the drag show and from Cathedral. He was sitting across the beige living room of Sarah, a Queen Bee lesbian theology student cum- stripper who called herself the "Main Gay" of Bloomington, at a party consisting of mostly women and trans men, vodka and cranberry juice, a late-night order of cheese bread with garlic butter dipping sauce cooling on the coffee table, and a barely audible episode of *Xena: Warrior Princess* on the television. I can't explain how I knew he was important just sitting there. Most words I use to describe it sound mystical, but it wasn't. There have been a few people in my

---

14. This is a coincidence and is not meant to suggest a relationship between Carrie/ Caleb and the Owen composite character from the author's romantic history.

life I've known were going to be important to me just by looking at them. Caleb was one. That's all.

He made some witty joke, I remember, and I laughed, and at some point we started talking. Caleb was not a photographer then. He hadn't even thought of becoming a photographer. He had dropped out of a Master's program in Sociology and was working as a writing tutor at IU while Leyna finished her Master's Degree in Marketing. When I met him, Caleb called himself a writer. We talked enough to discover that both of us were working on novels. Mine was about vampire lesbian strippers. His was about his mother's death.

I asked him if he'd like to be novel-writing-buddies, and he said yes, so we started talking about art. That fall, though, he abandoned his novel and decided to try his hand at visual art instead. He used some of the money his mother had left him to buy some nice camera equipment and began taking pictures of his friends—Leyna, Sarah, Thade, me.

Around that winter, we started talking about Art with a big "A." By that spring, Caleb knew he was going to go to photography school in Boston, and Thade knew he didn't want to go to Boston. Caleb's and my friendship immediately intensified, since for all we knew, come September, we'd be hundreds of miles away from one another. I cut my hair into a faux-hawk to look like more like him. I started wearing pants with collared shirts and vests, partially because I was really into Bob Dylan circa 1966 and partially because Caleb said he liked how I looked in them.

That summer we both quit our jobs so we could spend more time together making art. We would pass long afternoons in each other's living rooms mod podging collages on the carpet. We started using the word Love about each other. Before September, when he left for Boston with Leyna and I left for Europe with Thade, Caleb and I got married.

Chapter Eleven
Poetesse Dijonaise

*D*ifferent regions in France have specific etiquette around the number of cheek-bisous you're supposed to give female friends when you say hello and goodbye. The general rule is the more rural you get, the more kisses. In bustling Paris, you just do two, one for each cheek. In Paris also it's young and hip for guys, gay or straight, to greet close guy friends with bisous. When I saw this happen I thought it was cool and kind of hot. In Normandy, they do four, and saying hello or goodbye to a large group of friends can take several minutes. In the mid-sized, Gothic college town of Dijon, it's three.

There was just enough mist to pixilate the light around the Dijon streetlamps. To our right, a dim boulangerie sheltered a group of boisterous students from the January chill. Julian and Caleb hunched under the weight of their luggage while I texted a girl named Lucile who was supposed to pick us up. We had dragged our bags around the entire circumference of the train station because of a miscommunication caused by two hotels of the same name within walking distance of one another. I was limping and getting cranky because of the pain in my left leg. It always hurt worse when it was wet outside, and I'd been dragging my own bag because everyone was equally cranky with hunger and I felt bad asking Julian to do it again.

Two girls appeared out of the haze, one riding the other piggy-back. They both smile-laughed as the bottom one strutted up the sidewalk. Both were in their early-to-mid-twenties and conspicuously pretty, with Renaissance-painting figures and near-phosphorescent skin. When they were about twenty meters away, the top one pointed at us, and the bewitching bicephalus strode in our direction.

As they approached, the top one hopped off without waiting for the bottom one to slow down, both still smile-laughing. The one who'd been on top had sienna skin with a tight mass of curly, dark hair. The one who'd been on bottom had milky skin with straight blond hair tied back in a ponytail and glasses with thick, green plastic frames.

The top one stuck out her hand to me and said, *Hello, I'm Brigitte.*

I shook her hand. *Salut, Brigitte. Je m'appelle Jade.*

Hello, Jade, said Brigitte.

Then the bottom one stuck out her hand to Julian and said, *Hello, I'm Lucile,* and Julian shook her hand and said, *Hi, I'm Julian.*

Hello, Julian, said Lucile.

Hello, Julian, said Brigitte.

They both looked at Caleb, and he said, with Anglophonic pronunciation, *Sa-loo. Je m'appelle Caleb.*

Lucile and Brigitte looked at one another, then back at Caleb. *Kale?* asked Brigitte.

Caleb blushed. *Caleb,* he repeated, *Cay-leb.*

Cay-lem? said Lucile.

Caleb makes a certain face when he doesn't know what to say. He looks at me and then down to one side and sort of grimaces with half his mouth. He made that face and shrugged.

Caleb, I said as clearly as I could. *Il s'appelle Caleb.*

Caleb? she said, looking at him.

Wee, he said.

Ah, très bien. Bonsoir, Caleb.

Bon swar.

D'accord, on y va! said Lucile. *Est-ce que c'est ton bagage?*

Oué, I said. She took the handle of my suitcase and started dragging it toward the parking lot.

In the car, Brigitte and Lucile spoke to each other in French in the front seat while the three Americans sat in the back. Brigitte looked over her shoulder and said something too fast and complicated for me to understand. She tried again and when I made a confused face, she said, *You are hungry?*

Oh, yeah. I mean, oué. On a faim. Right guys?

Julian and Caleb nodded.

What would you like to eat? Lucile said, glancing back through the rearview mirror.

I don't care, as long as it's fast and cheap, said Julian, leaning against the window.

Kebabs? said Brigitte.

Sure. He made an exasperated hand gesture that was obviously meant to be seen while looking like it wasn't meant to be seen.

Lucile said something else to Brigitte that I didn't catch.

Oh yes, said Brigitte. *Dareka a dit que vous voulez acheter du vin?*

Er, pardon? Plus lentement, s'il te-plait?

Brigitte looked at Lucile.

One of you would like to search for some wine?

Oh! Oui, I said. *C'est vrai. C'est moi!*

I turned to Caleb and Julian. *I mentioned to Dareka that Burgundy was my favorite type of wine. I guess he told them that.*

We have a friend who is just finished at her work, said Lucile. *She will take you, if you like.*

The buildings were all centuries-old stone, hardly any taller than two or three stories. We drove through the light drizzle for only a few minutes before Lucile pulled onto a side street and parked. The three Americans followed the French girls out of the car and into a chic bistro with high tables and black lacquer chairs that could have been in Harvard Square except for everything being in French.

It was about 19:00h, and the restaurant was about half-full, mostly with people drinking wine. I was getting lightheaded from hunger and started to read the menu that was written in chalk on a blackboard above the bar.

When I looked back toward Caleb to ask if he knew what "andouillette" was, there was a tall, chestnut-haired young woman standing beside him. She looked like a cross between Milla Jovovich, Audrey Hepburn, and Snow White, with pale skin and the lightest splash of freckles across her nose and cheeks.

Lucile was standing to my right. She must have said something, but I didn't hear her speak. After a period of silence during which I stared stupidly at the girl in front of me, Caleb said, *I think she said we can either go with her and Brigitte and get food, or we can go with Adélaïde and look for some wine.*

Adélaïde smiled, one dimple asymmetrically accenting perfect, makeup-less features.

Can we go with Adélaïde? I said, looking at Caleb.

Caleb shrugged and made that face. *Sure.*

I turned to Lucile. *On va aller avec Adélaïde. Est-ce que c'est d'accord?*

She said, *Ouais, absolument,* followed by a long, facial-expression-heavy string of rapid French.

Adélaïde raised her dark eyebrows. *D'accord,* she said in a rich, smoky voice. *Attendez un moment. Il faut que je pointe.* She looked right at me and winked before turning on her toes to disappear.

Lucile motioned for us to follow her outside where Brigitte was standing by the car smoking home-rolled cigarettes with Julian.

Caleb and I are going to go wine shopping with Lucile's friend, I said. *I think you can come with us or go with Lucile and Brigitte.*

Julian took a drag and pushed the damp flaxen hair back from his forehead as if he were being filmed. *I don't care what I do as long as I get something to eat and a shower. I'm famished, I'm filthy, and I still stink of Amsterdam.*

I did my best to work out with Lucile and Brigitte between my expressionist French and their Hollywood English that Julian was going to go with them, and Caleb, Adélaïde, and I would meet them later at the venue and that it was okay for us to leave our baggage in their car. I gave them each a copy of the chapbook I'd made for the tour—five of my poems in both English and French. They both said, in English, *Thank you.*

Adélaïde walked toward us in a black trench coat, black fedora, and cowboy boots. Her hair cascaded from under the hat and fell like a thick cape just around her shoulders.

Ready? she said.

Yes! I said. *I mean, oui. On y va.*

I bisou'd Lucile and Brigitte and then they bisou'd an off-guard, nervous Caleb and took off with Julian, red taillights glowing in the mist.

So you want to buy some wine? Adélaïde said, rising slightly on her toes with the inflection of her sentence.

Oué. Peut être. Si c'est bon.

She brought an index finger to her lips, then snapped her fingers. *Yes, I know just the shop.* We followed her purposed pace down damp side streets until we came to a well-lit thoroughfare. Late-adolescents were everywhere grabbing kebabs and pastries before heading off to their evening plans. It was just like the main street of my and Caleb's college town grafted onto toits bourguignons[15] instead of Indiana limestone.

The wine shop was a small boutique with a middle-aged male clerk whom Adélaïde greeted with small-town familiarity. We stood in front of a rack of Burgundy wine, the three of us in a row in order of height, Adélaïde to me down to Caleb.

What type of wine do you like? she asked. *White? Red?*

Rouge, I said. *Et pas très cher.*

She brought her finger to her lips again, then extended it toward a bottle at eyelevel.

This one is not bad, she said, with a tiny shrug. *Thirteen euros is not the best price, but the wine is good. As well, we could go to a supermarket if this is too expensive. The wine there will be cheap.*

I picked up the bottle and turned it over in my hands. I only had carry-on luggage with me, which meant I couldn't fly any bottles home, and Caleb didn't really drink.

J'aime ton chapeau, I said, putting the bottle back on the shelf.

Oh, thank you, she said, pulling down the rim of the black felt fedora. *Do you think it makes me look like Humphrey Bogart?*

Um, do you want to look like Humphrey Bogart?

I would be glad to look like him if it means I can act like him.

---

15. I didn't know this term when I was there. I didn't even know if the architecture was Gothic, Renaissance, or what. I only saw old, romantic stone and multicolored tile roofs reflecting streetlights through the mist.

Oh, you're an actor?

Yes.

And a poet?

Yes.

Are you going to read at the show tonight?

I think so. You have made a choice?

Oh, yeah. I looked back at the wall of red wine. Caleb was standing to my right, clutching his large camera bag to his hip.

Thank you so much for bringing us here, I said, *but I actually don't think there's any way for me to bring this back with me. When I told Dareka I loved Burgundy, I was thinking more of just drinking a glass of wine somewhere.*

She nodded with a pronounced frown and shrug that meant *Je comprends,* and said, *Well, let's go then.*

She said au revoir to the clerk and we were back outside. The road was blocked off for pedestrian use, so we lingered in the middle of the street. It was night completely now. The only lights came from the shops' windows and signs and the streetlamps. The first thing she did when we stopped walking was pull a tissue out of her coat pocket and blow her nose.

So you want to go to a bar? she said while digging out the insides of both nostrils.

I looked at Caleb and he made that face.

Actually, would you like to just show us around the town? We're only going to be here tonight, and I've never been to Dijon before. Maybe Caleb can take some pictures.

A tour?

Yes! I looked at Caleb. *What do you think?*

He made that face again and looked down. *Um, I'm fine doing whatever.*

Adélaïde smiled and rose up on her toes. *Okay, yes. Let's go.* She turned and started walking down a small cobblestone alley. As we followed her silhouette—fedora to trench coat to slender knees to boots—I looked at Caleb, clutched both hands in front of my sternum, and mouthed, *Oh. My. God.* He shook his head and took his camera out of its bag.

Okay, she said as we stepped out of the alley and onto another main street. *I'm going to show you the places in Dijon I love. Sounds good?*

Sure! Et, alors. Tu peux parler en français, s'il te plait, I said. *Je dois m'entraîner.*

She nodded. *Okay. Je vais faire le guide en français, si c'est bon.*

Oué.

The four wooden heels of Adélaïde's and my cowboy boots clopped like horse hooves on the flat stone streets. The air was crisp but much more inviting than that of New England's icy January. My suede coat and leather gloves kept me comfortable, and the rain, which cycled rhythmically from haze to drizzle to spray, was refreshing after spending five hours on a train. She led us down twisting roads and alleys, injecting odd facts and comments about the shops and cafés we passed. I understood about one-third of what she said but nodded and said *oué* and *intéressant* frequently. We walked past a freestanding gate that looked like a miniature Arc de Triomphe, and she took another tissue out of her coat pocket and blew her nose again.

Est-ce que tu es malade? I asked.

She shook her head and touched her nose. *Toujours.*

I heard Caleb chuckle, then I heard his camera's shutter click.

We walked into an ovular courtyard in front of a sweeping, alighted building that looked like, and was, a palace. Adélaïde told us that, like the Louvre and many other architectural relics of outdated royalty, it had been turned into an art museum.

Mais à Dijon, nous sommes surtout célèbres pour nos églises. On y va.

She started walking briskly again, pointing to dark structure looming over the other rooftops. *C'est là que nous allons. Notre Dame.*

We walked. Caleb lingered behind us to take photos of me and Adélaïde in our cowboy boots shrouded in the mist between the mythic structures, and I tried not to think of fairytales. These buildings were real. Practical. Designed and built by human beings for human needs. The Gothic and Renaissance architecture had seen generations through war and disease and invention. Our breathing and eating in these walls was living palimpsest. We were writing our stories over the stories of the past.

I tried to keep pace with Adélaïde without limping or stopping. My left leg was starting to cramp, but I wouldn't ask her to slow down. When we reached the church she'd pointed out, we stopped in front of an ominous, locked gate. Mounted next to the gate, just high enough so that Caleb would need to stand on his tiptoes to reach it, was a Chihuahua-sized statue of an owl.

Adélaïde gestured to the owl and said something in French, then touched the statue with her left hand while gazing pensively at another church spire that rose over the rooftops. After a few moments, she inhaled deeply and withdrew her hand, then she walked a few steps and turned away from us as if she were waiting politely for us to change clothes.

I think we're supposed to make a wish, I said to Caleb.

Caleb looked at the statue and bit his bottom lip. He moved his camera over to his right hip, stood on his toes, and reverently touched the stone bird. His eyes found the same church spire Adélaïde's had, and for a moment, we both held our breath and everything became still. Caleb almost looked like a statue himself.

Then he exhaled back onto his heels and brought his left hand back to the camera at his hip. He stepped back and waited for me to make my wish.

I looked at the owl, which, because of its cuteness, I was pretty sure wasn't technically a gargoyle. I'd made hundreds of wishes in my life over fetishes of magical thinking—birthday candles, Virgin Mary apparitions, penny-filled fountains, Mardi Gras beads blessed by Voodoo priestesses, etc. Most of these wishes after age thirteen had been variations on *Please [God, Abyss, Shiva, Avalokiteshvara, St. Teresa of Avila, Thoth, Orpheus, Pallas Athena, Ghost of William Faulkner, Bar Where Ernest Hemmingway Drank Once, Other Symbolic Deity], let me be a writer.* This time, though, that standby didn't feel appropriate. I was on tour in Europe being paid to perform my poetry. Just because my being a writer looked more like reading in dive bars and cafés than schmoozing with Oprah didn't mean my wish hadn't come true. Any symbolic deity hearing me wish, at this point, to be a writer, would, I expected, determine me ungrateful.

I took a deep breath, touched the owl with my left hand, looked at the spire, and said, in my head, *I wish that both Caleb and I have a good year.* (I'd found that for me, when it came to things like prayer and New Year's Resolutions, vagueness was more effective than specificity.)

We rejoined Adélaïde.

I have a thought, she said, touching her bottom lip with her index finger. *Do you like to go to a restaurant where you can eat eggs poached in red wine?*

I looked at Caleb. He shrugged and made a face that said, *I'm incredibly hungry, and I'll go anywhere you want.*

Oué, fantastique, I said. *On a beaucoup de faim.*

Great! I am taking you to my favorite restaurant in Dijon. Not too expensive. Fifteen euro perhaps and that is with wine.

That sounds amazing. I mean, fantastique.

If it pleases you, we can speak English now. It's good to practice English for me, too.

D'accord. I mean, okay.

We followed her through a large square in front of another imposing Gothic church. *Do you know Patti Smith?* Adélaïde said.

Caleb looked at me and let out a single, quiet chuckle that was more of a statement than a laugh.

Yeah, I said. *She's one of our all-time favorites.*

Adélaïde pointed at the church. *She play here two years ago, and I saw.* She held her right hand over her heart in a loose fist. *She is my mother. I mean, my mother who I didn't know. You understand?*

Yes, je comprends. She's one of my heroes. Caleb and I saw her a couple of years ago in Providence. She wore cowboy boots just like yours. That's why I bought my cowboy boots.

She stopped in the middle of the street and looked down at both of our footwear as though she only just noticed the coincidence. *Oh, so we two are sisters, after all.* She smiled at me. Her eyes were warm brown and looking at them for too long embarrassed me, so I glanced up at her hat.

This looks like the start of a beautiful friendship, I said.

Oh! she said. *You quote Mr. Bogart from one of my favorite movie. It's terrible how unknown is Casablanca in France. That's such a pity! So I'm glad you did so because no one else here would do.*

I heard the click of Caleb's camera. I looked back at him and his camera looked at me and clicked again.

Chapter Twelve
Portraits

For six years, Caleb and I have collaborated on an extended portrait project. It started in Bloomington the summer of 2006, right before he moved to Boston and I went to Europe with Thade.

Caleb and I spent a lot of time that summer at each other's houses developing high-concept art pieces with varying success rates. One involved handwritten letters by fictional people expressing their loneliness and need for human connection, signed with pleas for any sort of written response. Each envelope contained another envelope stamped and addressed to a PO box we'd rented. We would leave the letters in strategic places, like coffee shops and libraries, and we always disguised our handwriting. We checked the PO box once a week, but no responses ever came.

Other projects were more successful, such as shellacking collages of fashion magazines and pornography. We came up with the mantra *EVERYTHING'S GOING TO BE OKAY* and wrote it in sharpie in every bathroom stall we visited in Bloomington. I also came up with the slogan *ART SAVES,* inspired by the many Christian billboards and bumper stickers in Southern Indiana. We had ART SAVES stickers printed up and stuck them everywhere[16].

We talked a lot about artists we loved, especially Patti Smith and Robert Mapplethorpe. Even more than their work, we loved their story. How Patti Smith moved to New York from New Jersey to become an artist. How their working relationship carried them through a young romance that evolved to a mature romantic friendship. How much they loved each other. How they were so, so queer[17].

As far as the portraits, we never decided to do it. It just happened and kept happening. Caleb decided he wanted to become a photographer, and he started shooting me. He didn't know what he was doing yet. He was learning and I was his test subject.

One of my favorite pictures of me ever is me in Bloomington's old, Southern-feeling graveyard. I'm leaning against a headstone that's a large crucifix with an eroding Jesus, looking out past the viewer. I'm 23 and have short, dyed-black hair. There's a lit cigarette in my mouth, but I didn't smoke[18].

A portrait is really a picture of the relationship between the artist and the model. That's why the Mapplethorpe photos of Patti Smith are so striking. No one knew her like him and no one knew him like her and the real picture is that knowing.

At the end of the summer Caleb knew he was moving to Boston and I didn't know for sure what I was going to do, so we had an Art Marriage ceremony at the anarchist co-op bookstore to profess our profound Art commitment and also our real, nonphysical undying Love. It was a Friday evening event. We flyered and advertised and

---

16. I even brought some with me on my first trip to Europe in 2006. As far as I saw, none of them survived to 2012.

17. I don't know if Patti Smith has ever self-identified as queer. That didn't matter so much to me in 2006, since I wasn't always certain if I did either.

18. Patti Smith didn't smoke either. There's a famous photo of her by Mapplethorpe holding a lit cigarette. For this, Mapplethorpe reportedly called her a "poseur."

invited everyone we knew. About sixty people came to see exhibits of all the work we'd created over the summer, hear me read some poems, and watch us get married. We wrote our own vows and exchanged vials of fake blood. Thade performed the ceremony and Caleb's girlfriend, Leyna, was the vial-bearer.

Caleb and Leyna had been together for three years and Thade and I had been together for four years. Caleb had asked Leyna if it was okay with her that we got Art Married because he and Leyna knew they were going to get married for real in the next couple of years[19]. She said it was. I didn't ask Thade if it was okay with him, but I'm almost positive he would have said it was if I had.

Thade and I knew we weren't going to get married for real. Thade wanted to stay in Indiana near his family and live a simple life teaching piano and probably eventually go to grad school. I wanted to go to a real city on a coast and be an artist. Thade[20] said I could be an artist in Bloomington, and I said not the kind of artist I wanted to be.

I passed out on Leyna and Caleb's couch after pints of whiskey and hours of repetitive dialogue about what I should do romance- and moving-wise more than a few nights that summer. In the end, I moved to Boston and that was the end of me and Thade.

In Boston, I was Caleb's model throughout his stay at photography school. When I started performing, he took all of my pictures. Over the next five years, the portraits continued, trudging through the snow against an eye-blue sky; under streetlights in knee-high boots, push-up bra, and lip-liner; makeupless in a grey polo-dress with an electro-shock hair tangle; giddily nude in hungover, post-sex, bedroom

---

19. Thade performed that ceremony too, and I performed a poem which I'd written for Luke (of all people) and modified to be about Leyna and Caleb. It had been about a year and a half since Thade and I'd broken up. We did not speak.

20. Because it rhymed with Thade and because I knew I would want to bring some part of him and me with me was the least important of the excessive number of reasons why I later chose the name Jade. More important reasons will be explored in the chapter: "Jade is a Jade is a Jade is a Jade."

languor; autumn afternoon in a collared shirt, vest, and cowboy boots; drinking whiskey or eating ice cream sandwiches or doing absent-minded yoga poses in cut-offs in the back yard. We don't talk about why we do the portraits. It's just what we do.

When I post photos we've taken together on Facebook I usually tag Caleb. There are a lot more photos of me than of him on his page. There are a lot more of me than of anyone else.

Caleb uses a lot of our photos in the photography classes he teaches. He said recently he wonders if people wonder who I am. *My students know I'm married,* he said. *But then I've got all these pictures of this other woman.* I told him it was good for an artist to have intriguing interpersonal relationships.

I worked as an artist's model for years in my mid-twenties when I was broke. I had thousands of photos of me taken by dozens of photographers. Caleb's are the only ones I liked and still like. Caleb's are the only ones I can look at and see someone that looks at all how I think I am.

Chapter Thirteen
Poseurs

When we arrived at L'Epicerie & Cie, Adélaïde ordered a half-carafe of red wine, which the waiter brought out along with our menus and a basket of baguette. The restaurant was nearly empty and remarkably rustic with exposed stone walls, rounded, hut-like, ceilings, wooden tables and chairs, and an open kitchen. In Cambridge, I would have thought a restaurant like this was trying too hard, but here, it felt authentic. I was aware of the fact that I assumed its authenticity mostly because I was in France and wasn't sure what that meant about me, France, or authenticity, if it meant anything at all.

Moments after the wine and bread were on the table, we heard the obtrusive vibration of a cell phone, and Adélaïde reached into her bag. *Excuse me, one moment,* she said. She held her phone to her ear, covered the other ear with her finger, and said, *Allô.* Caleb took a picture of her like that, curled over her cell phone with dark hair falling over her eyes. In a moment, her face lit up and she started speaking rapidly in French. Then, she stood and looked at us apologetically. *Just one moment,* she said. Leaving her coat and bag on her chair across from us, she walked outside. I poured three glasses of wine (a very shallow one for Caleb) while he tore off a piece of bread and buttered it. He shoved two-thirds of the buttered piece into his mouth and started to chew as if he were in an instructional video for those wishing to maximize their bread consumption efficiency and minimize their entanglement with all things not consuming bread.

How long do we have till the show? he said, covering his still-chewing mouth with his hand. *I thought they said it started at nine, and it's after eight-thirty.* He swallowed and shoved the rest of the bread in his hand into his mouth, then tore off another piece and started buttering.

She's got it. She's going to the show, so she knows when we need to get there.

I just don't want you to be late.

I know. Thank you.

I ripped my paper napkin in half, placed half on my lap, and used the other half to blow my nose. Caleb started in on his second piece of bread, and I sipped my wine. It tasted especially crisp and balanced, as I was aware I expected it to because I was in a rustic restaurant in Burgundy drinking Burgundy and not on a back porch in Jamaica Plain drinking Trader Joe's wine out of a souvenir coffee mug.

So, I said. *She's ridiculous.*

Caleb covered his chewing mouth. *Yeah, but how old is she though?*

Twenty-five. She said that, didn't you hear? In French right before we got to that gargoyle thing we wished on.

I guess I missed it.

She said, 'J'ai habité en Dijon depuis veingt-cinq ans, et je l'aime,' or something like that.

I believe you.

Twenty-five is perfectly reasonable, isn't it?

Yeah, totally fine.

And she's ridiculous.

No, she is. There are lots of people with great personalities, and there are lots of beautiful people[21], and she, legitimately, is both.

I sipped my wine and tore myself a small piece of baguette. For a moment, both Caleb and I were silent except for the quiet breath and saliva noises of eating. Adélaïde reentered smiling with her entire being. She told us she'd just gotten a job working on a movie set in Paris. It meant spending four days a week in Paris for three months, starting the following Monday. She had a friend with an extra room in the city where she could stay for free.

It is not acting, but it is in the film industry, and I believe Paris will be inspirating for my writing.

I'm sure it will be, I said. *That's what Paris does. Congratulations.*

I held up my wine glass, and we all toasted her new job. Adélaïde sipped the wine and made a face of discernment, as if she were assessing her choice, then nodded to herself and placed the glass back down. Caleb took the tiniest sip possible. I drank uncritically. Adélaïde took a tissue out of her pocket and blew her nose.

Three small plates of salad and toast arrived, along with three smooth burnt sienna earthenware pots holding poached eggs floating embryonically in deep ruby-purple broth. Caleb's face dropped when he saw bits of ham floating in the sauce.

Oh crap. You can't eat that, can you? I said.

---

21. Caleb has often made sly references to the fact that I tend to exclusively date and be interested in notably physically attractive people. I did not realize or acknowledge this was true until I was twenty-eight and found myself following Leigh back to her apartment under the pretense of songwriting two days after she'd smoked crack and gotten a matching tattoo that said *Badville* on her inner thigh with a bearded, bike-riding bass-player whom she'd dated and broken up with in four separate explosions of dishonesty in the past six months. *This woman is insane,* I thought as she shooed her roommate's puggle off her frameless twin mattress and peeled off her pants. She was, but she also looked like Arwen the Elf Princess as played by the impossible brunette lovechild of Edie Sedgwick and Brigitte Bardot.

Caleb shrugged and shook his head. *No. It's okay. I knew this was going to happen here.*

Yeah, when I was here six years ago, I was a vegetarian. I basically lived off of crêpes and croque-madames.

There is a problem with the eggs? said Adélaïde, who was already dipping a toast corner into a golden yolk.

Caleb's a vegetarian.

Oh? He does not eat eggs?

Eggs are okay, but there's ham in it. See those little pink bits?

She squinted at her bowl. *Oh, I see. Well, maybe there is something else.* She reached for the menu and started to scan it. *Yes, here is onion soup?*

That all has a beef base, Caleb said. *It's really okay. I knew this was going to happen. I'll just eat bread and find something later. A crêpe or something.*

Here, take my salad. I took the ceramic dish off my plate and gave him the small pile of greens. I also gave him my two thick slices of toast smeared with salted butter. He wound up eating that and the rest of the complimentary baguette in the center of the table. I finished his eggs and most of his wine.

Oh, said Adélaïde, glancing at the Roman numerals of the large, old-looking clock on the brick wall across from her. *It's time.*

We paid the bill and followed our guide back out into the street where the mist had solidified into intermittent drops of cold rain. She walked quickly. My left leg was cramping, and I struggled to keep up without a noticeable limp. We crossed a street into a wide courtyard where Adélaïde waved and smiled at a dark-haired, dapper, five-o'clock-shadowed young man walking in the other direction. The two greeted one another and bisou'd, and I felt weirdly jealous. Then, I reminded myself that kissing, in France, is as platonic a greeting as a hug would be back on the streets in Cambridge, and that I was being creepy, and that I was supposed to be abstinent right now, anyway.

When the young man left, flashing a smile, Adélaïde turned to us and curled her lip. *That guy is a creep,* she said, narrowing her eyes as she watched him walk away.

Oh really? I said. *What makes him a creep?*

She was still glaring out the corner of her eye. *He dated a friend of mine. She was away, and he slept with another girl, and after he is saying, 'What is wrong? You were not inside the country. I didn't know that this was not all right.'*

I laughed too loud. *Ah, yes. You have to love that one. 'What did I do wrong? You never said I wasn't supposed to sleep with other people!'*

She looked at us. *You mean guys in the U.S. do this too?*

Oh yeah, said Caleb. *Guys everywhere do.*

She considered this for a moment. *That's too bad,* she said, and started walking again. *I was hoping the U.S. was the Promised Land.*

Caleb and I hurried after her.

There's a lot more in the U.S. than guys, I said.

Yes, I'm sure, she said. *I've never been. One day I will go.* She looked back at me. *You are in Boston?*

Yes.

She nodded. *I see. Well, Boston is now on my To Travel list.*

We passed the town's Cathedral on our way, and Adélaïde slowed, turned, and began to walk backwards as she resumed her tour-guide role. *That is Cathedral Saint Bénigne. Last year, I performed in a great theatre festival here with poets, dance, some Japanese-type puppets. I did some Butoh. Do you know the discipline? It was very inspirating.* She gestured to the building's facade. *You see the stones? They have, how do you say it, nettoyage?*

Cleaned? said Caleb.

Yes. The government was cleaned the outside of the Cathedral last year. It used to be very dark, not light like this. She raised a hand toward the ashen arches.

You don't like it? I said.

She paused and touched her lip. *I think, when things are old, they should look old.*

Chapter Fourteen
Other People's Clothes

*I*n 2008, while I was dating Luke[22], Caleb asked if he could come over and wear my clothes for his final project at the New England School of Photography. I said sure, anything you want.

He came over in the afternoon and raided my closet to take a self-portrait for his series, *Other People's Clothes*. I left him alone and stayed in the kitchen doing dishes. That was a period when I was sick all the time. I wasn't eating well, and most healthcare officials probably would have classified me as an alcoholic. In the photo, Caleb's wearing a trendy, dress-length hoodie and skinny jeans and pretending to blow dry his faux-hawk. On my desk, you can see my laptop, a box of Thin Mint Girl Scout Cookies, and a handle of Jim Beam.

Other People's Clothes was a series of self-portraits of Caleb wearing other people's clothes, with other people's stuff, in other people's spaces. In each photograph, he created and embodied a different character, using his androgynous appearance and theater background to his advantage.

---

22. This was the height of my femmiest phase, when I would regularly do full makeup and put on heels to do things like go to the drugstore or catch a 7AM flight.

The series took off. It was shown in galleries across the country and appeared in journals and magazines all over the world. Caleb became instantly cool in the self-conscious, self-referential Boston arts scene. He was in all the dailies and weeklies. People in the street would recognize him regularly. I told him he was famous, and he told me he wasn't[23].

In 2010, I walked up the steps of the Broadway T station on my way to Caleb's first major solo art opening for *OPC* in a South End gallery. I wore a collared shirt and vest and so did he. Mine were black and grey. His were purple and fuchsia.

As I walked into the space, I realized that at some point I'd failed to notice, we'd stopped aspiring. We'd moved beyond dress-up games in Midwestern living rooms and had grown into the clothes of working artists.

---

23. My first book of poetry was published in 2009. Shortly after, I began touring some of the nation's biggest poetry venues, and I became instantly cool. As this happened, Caleb told me I was famous, and I told him I wasn't.

Chapter Fifteen
Nom de Scène

The bar was packed with clusters of people lingering outside in dark coats, attempting to avoid the light rain by cramming all[24] of their bodies underneath the temporary metal scaffolding that umbrella'd the sidewalk as they smoked their home-rolled cigarettes. Standing cigaretteless among the damp smokers was Dareka. When he saw us he waved. We walked over, and he and I bisou'd.

Dareka's real name was Marc, but in the poetry world he went by Dareka Daremo, which was Japanese for Somebody Nobody[25]. I met Dareka when he was studying in Boston a couple of years earlier, and I impressed him with my grade school French and with the Japanese I'd picked up during the period in my teens when the only music I listened to was J-pop soundtracks to shoujo anime series. We had several broken, tri-lingual barroom conversations during this epoch in which I told him the following: one, I had gone to college in Indiana, which was a state near Chicago; two, I had spent some time in Paris and had

---

24. Even with European notions of personal space, this was not quite an achievable task.

25. French pen/stage names were way cooler than American. Other favorites were (in translation): Molotov Cocteau, Mister Lady, and Spring 2004.

enjoyed it; and three, my heart/soul/mind approached tomorrow's sky on wings of an angel. Then, I would nod and say, *hai wakatta,* or, *oué, je comprends,* after whatever he said. Dareka looked almost satirically French. Slender, slightly slouched frame, prominent nose, and a dark, sculpted mustache.

Jade! Yes, I'm glad you are here. Julian is inside. I talked to Bernard. He will give you each two slots, one at the beginning of the night, and one at the end. And you know, I told you, I think, that this night has no pay, but it is a show in between Amsterdam and Reims, and you can sell your books if you like.

Oui, je sais. C'est d'accord. Dareka, c'est Caleb Cole, mon ami, le photographe.

Caleb extended a tense right hand to shake Dareka's and said, *Bon swar.* Dareka shook his hand and, thankfully, did not try to bisou.

Cole? Nice to meet you. My name is Marc, or Dareka in poetry. I'm happy you could come. Did you have a nice flight?

Um, it was long. But it was fine.

Caleb hasn't slept in about twenty-four hours, I said.

Yeah, Caleb said. *But it's fine. I knew this would happen.*

I looked for Adélaïde, but she was gone.

You want to go inside and sit down? I said to Caleb.

Caleb shrugged. *Sure. I mean, whatever.*

Yes, said Dareka. *We are along the side. I'll come with you and introduce you to Bernard.*

The large barroom swarmed with attractive, artistic-looking young people in scarves and engaging hats. Along the right side of the wall was a long table where Julian sat resting his chin on his palm in between Lucile and Brigitte. Dareka introduced me to about fifteen different people whose names I had no hope of remembering.

You see there? He pointed at a tall, slender man with a short, dark beard. *That is Bernard. Come with me, and I'll introduce you. Actually, do you want to sit down? Here, come sit down first. Put down your things, and then I will take you to meet Bernard.*

Julian looked relaxed and greeted me with an exaggeratedly solicitous expression and an extended hug. *How was dinner?* he asked, blond eyebrows lifting, *Good?* I had been around him long enough to know that after periods of crankiness Julian had the tendency[26] to compensate with overboard performative consideration. Caleb promptly set up his camera and our bags in a smaller version of the stuff-fortress I'd found him in in Gare de Lyon. I didn't see Adélaïde anywhere.

Are you going to do the piece in French? asked Dareka. *I'm sorry we did not get to practice it much.*

I don't know, I said. *Maybe. If I do I might try to run through it a few times outside first.*

Either way is good, said Dareka. *Most here speak some English. They will be able to understand something[27]. Oh, I almost forgot, your bar coins. Here.*

He handed me two large wooden nickels, and I used one to buy a bright red beer in a large glass goblet that tasted like fermented apple. I caught my reflection in the mirror behind the bar. I was wearing a checked collared shirt and a black sweater vest with a small silver pin, which Caleb had given me two years earlier as a thank you for performing at his wedding. It was a handlebar mustache with the words *MUSTACHE RIDES: 5¢* along the bottom.

---

26. This pattern was easy to recognize because these were the same two interpersonal states my father had oscillated between my whole life.

27. I wasn't sure if I believed him. It was almost impossible for me to understand any of the French poetry I heard. In conversation, I could piece together most exchanges from context, but when words started playing around with expectations and connotations and metaphor, I found myself quickly in the dark. Add to that the undying French poetic affinity for surrealistic imagery, and it was hopeless.

I sat down at the table and saw Adélaïde's hat near the back of the room. I was about to stand up again when I was addressed by a tall and rather muppetly-postured young man with a floppy ash-brown bowl-cut sitting on the other side of Julian.

Hi, he said, with a prime-time-TV-worthy American accent, *I'm Scott.*

Hi, Scott, I said. *I'm Jade.*

You guys are American? he said, his voice and face carrying the dull excitement with which most American expats in Europe greet each other.

Yeah, I said. *And I assume so are you?*

He smiled big. *Yeah, I'm from Rhode Island. Where are you guys from?*

We live in Boston, I said, gesturing to Caleb and myself, *but we're originally from Indiana. Julian lives in New York, but he used to live in Boston.*

Well, I don't live anywhere, now, said Julian, tossing his bangs back from his forehead. *I'm on tour for the next five months.* His eyes affected a faraway gaze. *After that, who knoooows.*

Wow, said Scott. *You guys are on tour for five months?*

We're not, I said. *Caleb and I are going home after next week. Julian's going on forever and ever amen.*

Wow, Scott said again. *Then he looked at Caleb. You're a poet, too?*

Caleb shook his head. *No, I'm a groupie. I'm just here for her.* He pointed at me.

He's a photographer, I said.

Wow[28], like for a job? said Scott. *I'm just a student. I write for fun, but... wow.*

---

28. When we first arrived in Barcelona and Julian had declared to our host that he was "ecstatic" to perform at Poetry Slam Barcelona at Tinta Roja, Dareka rolled his eyes and remarked[†] that he was acting like a "typical American." One European stereotype

The poetry finally began, and Adélaïde took the stage. I was waiting for what Patti Smith and Robert Mapplethorpe called "The Magic." It was the feeling in Ralph's Diner on Halloween the night I read "On Breathing" and decided to come on this tour, and what I'd seen happen to Louis[29] the night we met at the Cantab. The air in the room changed, became more electric. The way people breathed changed. The whole room seemed to breathe together, steadily and continuously, all energy moving and being moved by everyone half-consciously in a rhythmic circle.

The Magic did not quite happen when Adélaïde performed, but at least the room grew quiet. Part-way through, she introduced a heavily-French-accented refrain of the English sentence, *My body is not a playground,* before launching into a broken English verse that was only slightly more intelligible to me than the French poetry.

I leaned over to Caleb. *If I look half as cute doing poetry in French as she does in English,* then I'll be fine.

I looked at Julian hunched over a four-inch chapbook of poems. He felt my gaze, looked up, and adjusted the square, plastic frames of his glasses. *These are his,* he mouthed to me while pointing to Scott, who smiled with all his teeth and shrugged in an aw-shucks kind of way.

I nodded and grinned, then I felt a hand on my shoulder. Dareka was letting us know that we were going up after the next poet.

I stood in front of the hundred or so bescarved poetry lovers. *Je suis très heureuse... uh... être ici,* I said. Then I read my poems.

---

about Americans was apparently that we were wide-eyed, emotionally hyperbolic, and somewhat naïve.

† *Ecstatic? Why are you ecstatic? Do you even know what that word means? You win one billion euros, then you are ecstatic. You fall into a swimming pool full with naked movie stars dipped in butter, then you are ecstatic. You find the cure for AIDS, then you are ecstatic. You perform at Tinta Roja, you are pleased, and you say, 'Thank you, I am going to perform,' and you do it.*

29. I found it strange that this was the first time I'd thought about Louis since I'd arrived in Europe, especially since just two weeks prior I was certain I was in love with him. I made a mental note to consider what this might mean about him and me or me and love.

When I sat back down, every fiber in my body was vibrating. I could feel eyes on me from all corners of the room. Caleb rested his camera on his lap and nodded at me. Julian mouthed *Good job,* and he meant it.

Julian performed, and the rest of the French poets, and before I knew it, we'd been there nearly four hours and the bar was starting to empty out. Julian was lost in whispered conversation with Scott, and Caleb was practically falling asleep.

Thank you for coming to France with me, I said to Caleb.

He perked up momentarily. *Sure. Thanks for giving me a reason to come.* He looked at his camera. *I think I got some good stuff.*

From across the room, I made eye-contact with Adélaïde. She smiled and waved at me from a crowd of fashionable, animated people. *I'm going to go mingle and try to sell some books,* I told Caleb, who I could tell was fading further from already-faded. Hopefully we won't be here too much longer.

It's fine, he said. *I knew this would happen.*

He followed me to where Adélaïde was standing, slumped against the bar.

J'ai aimé ta texte, I said to her.

She shrugged. *I don't know. It was okay. I liked very much yours though,* she said. *Your French, it is very good. I was thinking, I would like to have the text to look at.*

I reached into my bag and handed her one of the books. She took it gently.

Oh, this is in English? I am afraid I will not be able to understand. I have a book by William Blake, and I am so frustrating by all these brilliant words that are unpenetrative to me.

Non, non, I said, opening the book to the French section. *Les poèmes sont en anglais et fraînçais.*

She flipped through the French poems and smiled. *Oh, god bless you for that! I am always so frustrating by my English in the face of great poetry. Here, let me....* She placed the book on the bar as she began to open her purse and take out her wallet.

Non, non, non, I said, waving her wallet away. *C'est un cadeau. Pour... being our tour guide aujourd'hui.*

She smiled, looked again at the book, and tucked it into her bag along with the wallet. I was about to formulate something incisive to say in French when a stout man with full, wet lips and an enormous, bulldog-like head intercepted me.

Hey, that last poem you did, he said with a thick, British accent, *the one in English, I really appreciated it.*

Thank you, I said.

You said we could buy it?

Oh, yeah, here. I pulled out a few of my books and handed him one.

He turned it over in his hands without opening it. *Right. How much?*

I ask for a donation. Most people give around ten.

Ten?

Or thereabouts.

Right then. He reached into his pocket, took out his wallet, and handed me a twenty.

Hold on, and I'll get you change.

No, no, he said. *That's for you. That poem really meant something. It really said what I've always wanted to say.*

I looked in his eyes and took his hand. *Thank you,* I said. I tried to say it as earnestly as possible. *Are you a writer?*[30] I asked.

---

30. My go-to question at an event like this.

He shook his head. *No. I'm a rugby player for the Dijon team. I was traded down here last year. I hardly spoke a word of French at the time. Now, I speak about seven.* He laughed at his own joke. Then, he looked back at me.

It sure does get lonely sometimes, though.

Yes. I said.

The rugby player continued standing there for an uncomfortable period of time until I finally thanked him and turned back to Adélaïde, who had watched the whole thing from her tired slant. When the stocky Englishman finally left, I tried to continue our conversation, but I'd completely lost my train of thought. After a few attempts to say something remotely profound in French, I apologized for my mangling of her language.

It is okay, she said. *All poets speak the same language, and we do not like easy words.*

She was fingering a glass of pink wine[31]. In the mirror behind the bar, we looked like three half-deflated balloons.

Hey, do you want to hear a joke in English? said Adélaïde. It was a heroic attempt to enliven us.

Sure, said Caleb.

Wait, I said. *Let's film it for the internet. Hold on a second.* I handed Caleb my phone and he began recording. *Okay,* I said.

She composed herself and tried to contain her smirk. *Where do cows go on Friday night?*

Caleb and I paused for an appropriate moment before I said, *I don't know, where do cows go on Friday night?*

She raised her eyebrows and leaned into me. *To the moooooo-vies.*

---

31. I learned that this was not rosé wine but rather white wine mixed with cassis, which was a common Bourgogne drink.

She threw her head back with exaggerated cackling. The only verbal reaction I could muster was, *Oh.*

Lucile and Brigitte were bisouing Dareka and the rest of the crowd outside. Through the glass doors and huge windows, we watched as they scuttled off to the car across the street, got in, and drove away.

Those were the girls we're staying with, said Caleb.

Lucile said she's coming back, I said. *She's just driving Brigitte to some party. I think that's what she said, at least.*

Caleb made that face.

My bed can fit two, if you need, said Adélaïde. *There's also a couch, for the other.* Her attention was quickly hijacked by a man and woman— presumably a couple—who took hold of her arm and, giggling, dragged her off her stool several paces away and thrust an open book toward her face, pointing at some significant passage.

I looked at Caleb. *She just offered for me to sleep in her bed, didn't she?*

Yep.

I glanced at her out of the corner of my eye. She was holding the book now, and the couple watched like they were watching someone taste ice cream for the first time.

I can't, I said. *I'd never make a move, and I'd be too nervous to sleep. I'd just lie there all night worrying if I was breathing weird. Then I'd be all stiff in the morning and probably catch the flu, and I can't get sick now.*

Julian came in from outside, hair slightly disheveled, hands lifted as if he were clutching at air. *Oh my god. He went to Emerson. We have seven mutual friends!*

Wow, I said. *That's amazing.*

He grabbed both of my shoulders, eyes burning with electric romance. *I mean, what are the chances, right? We're in fucking Dijon. Like, where they make the mustard. Like, in France. And I meet someone from*

Emerson fucking College. He gripped harder. He looked into my eyes like he was trying to see the back of my skull.

I mean, he knows Casey fucking Rocheteau. Do you understand me, Jade? He let go of me and ran his hand through his hair and lifted his chin like he was presenting his best angle to a non-existent camera.

Busy, busy, busy[32], I said.

He sighed, blowing air out through his lips at an angle that lifted his blond bangs and gazing just slightly over my head.

He wants to come to Rome with me. There was a pause. He grabbed my shoulders again and brought his nose one inch from my nose. *Jade. He. Wants. To. Come. To. Rome. With. Me.*

That's great, I said. *You were worried about being there all alone.*

I know! It's perfect!

He let go again and sat momentarily on Adélaïde's empty stool. He leaned into the bar like Rock Hudson. *I just really needed something like this, you know? I was about at the end of my rope, what with Amsterdam and the money and everything. If this hadn't happened, I don't know what I'd've done. I really don't know what I'd've done, Jade.* He stood up and checked his chin-line in the mirror behind the bar. *I think he might be thirty percent crazy,* he said. *But sane people are boring, anyway. And besides, we'll be in Rome, so who gives a fuck?*

Scott poked his head back in the door, smiled, and waved at us. Julian waved back.

I'm going with him, he said, one hand on my shoulder. *I've already told Dareka. I'll be back at the apartment in time to catch the train tomorrow.* He squeezed once, let me go, and followed Scott out the door.

Adélaïde came back and reclaimed her seat. She listlessly pushed her rosy glass of wine toward me.

---

32. A Kurt Vonnegut reference I was pretty sure he didn't catch.

Here, do you want this? Somebody bought it for me. I did not even ask for it.

Thank you. I took a sip of the sweet drink. *Um, no thank you,* I said, and placed it back down on the bar between us.

She rested her elbow on the bar and her chin in her palm. *That guy, who your friend Julian did left with…* she said.

Yeah? Caleb said.

I was planning to give him my number.

Ten minutes later Lucile came back in, a whirl of awakeness.

Come! she said, taking my wrist. *Are you ready to go?*

Yes, I said. *We're exhausted.*

Oh, she said, looking slightly disappointed. *Well, that is okay. We have a room for you with a bed, just like we said. You may sleep if you like, though Dareka is coming over for a bit to hang out. We won't be too loud. Adé, will you come?*

Adélaïde looked at Caleb and me. *Will you hang out?* she asked.

I won't, said Caleb, then pointing at me, *but she might.*

I nodded. *I'll hang out for a little while.*

She sighed. *Okay, I will come for just a little bit.*

D'accord! said Lucile. *On y va!* She spun and led the way back out into the street, where we collected Dareka, and the five of us left the bar and its last lingering poets behind.

Chapter Sixteen
Le Corps Exquis

*Lights come up on LUCILE'S APARTMENT. Stage
right, JADE and CALEB stand with their baggage in
the guest bedroom in front of a small, white bed. Behind
the head of the bed is a single, square window with a half-
drawn white gauze curtain. Through the window, we see
the glow of streetlights through mist and the silhouette of a
church spire rising over flat rooftops. Stage left, LUCILE,
ADELAIDE, and DAREKA sit around a coffee table
with an ashtray talking while LUCILE rolls a joint.*

CALEB

So, I don't know if you have a side.

JADE

What?

CALEB

A side of the bed.

JADE

Oh, like, one I like?

CALEB

Yeah. Leyna usually takes the right. Right if you're looking at the bed, not if you're in it.

JADE

Audience right.

CALEB

Right.

JADE

I don't think I have a side. Let me think about it. No, I don't think I do. Do you want me to take audience right?

CALEB

It doesn't matter to me.

JADE

Well are you like, used to audience left, or do you want to change it up?

CALEB

[Shakes head. Shrugs.]

JADE

I'll take the right.

CALEB

[Turns his back to JADE and changes into pajama pants and a t-shirt]
I don't think I have any weird sleeping things. I don't snore. I don't
kick. I take up minimal room. I usually sleep on the edge, like curled
up in a little ball.

JADE

[Laughs.] I'm sure it'll be fine.

CALEB

[Gets into bed on the audience left side and pulls up the covers.] I have
to go to sleep. I'm sorry.

JADE

[Changes into pajamas—boxers and a Barcelona Poetry Slam t-shirt.]
Why are you sorry? That's some female-socialized bullshit. You
haven't slept in, what, twenty-four hours? You're fucking exhausted.
Don't be sorry.

CALEB

I know. I'm sorry.

We hear ADELAIDE laugh from the living room.

JADE

I'm going to go out with them, is that okay? I'll be quiet when I come
in.

CALEB

[From a huddled position in bed. We barely hear him.] That's fine.
Goodnight.

JADE

Thank you for coming to France with me.

CALEB

Sure.

JADE crosses into the living room and lights dim on the bedroom. She takes an empty seat around the coffee table. ADELAIDE and DAREKA sit across from each other upstage, right and left, respectively. LUCILE and JADE sit across from each other downstage, right and left, respectively. ADELAIDE is holding a notebook, which she occasionally scratches something in with a mechanical pencil. When JADE sits down LUCILE passes her a joint.

JADE

[Passes the joint to DAREKA.] Oh, non merci. Je n'aime pas beaucoup du... pot.

DAREKA

[Takes the joint and passes it to ADELAIDE without taking a hit.] Moi non plus. Merci quand même. [To ADELAIDE] Qu'est-ce que c'est?

ADELAIDE

[Takes the joint and holds it in her left hand, holding a pen in her right.] C'est un texte pour La Nuit du Slam en mars, à Toulouse. Ils avaient choisi dix poètes de différentes villes et leur ont demandé d'écrire un grand cadavre exquis. Ma partie était très difficile. Le dernier poète ayant participé, c'était Printemps Deux Mille Quatre. [She looks at the joint and shakes her head.] J'ai dit la semaine dernière que j'allais arrêter de fumer. [She takes a small hit.] D'accord, c'est tout pour moi. [She passes the joint to LUCILE.]

LUCILE

[Takes the joint and takes a hit.] Donne-moi ça, laisse-moi voir. [ADELAIDE hands her the notebook.] Bien dis donc, c'est vraiment difficile.

ADELAIDE

[Takes the notebook back from LUCILE, looks at it, folds her pencil into it, and places it on the table.]

DAREKA

C'est une bonne idée. Faisons un cadavre exquis maintenant.

LUCILE

Oui. D'accord. Avec l'américaine! Adé, on peut utiliser une pièce de ton carnet? [Hands the joint to JADE who passes it to DAREKA. For the rest of the scene, the joint moves counterclockwise around the circle, but the only one who drags is LUCILE.]

ADELAIDE

Sure. [Takes the pencil and tears a page out from her journal.] Qui veut commencer?

LUCILE

[Takes the pencil and paper and hands them to JADE.] Honneur à notre invitée.

JADE

Um. Quoi?

DAREKA

Do you know this game? Exquisite corpse?

JADE

Oh! Oué, oué, oué. Absolument. Je... used to do these at art parties in college. Je peut le commencer. [Takes the pencil and paper and starts to write.]

DAREKA

Est-ce que vous vous souvenez du poème de Printemps Deux Mille Quatre? Il l'a lu à Paris avec le Bon Slamaritain l'année dernière.

ADELAIDE

Oui! C'était un poème excellent. Mon ami qui n'aime pas la poésie l'a entendu, et après il m'a demandé 'Qu'est-ce que c'était ce poème de ce type? Je pense qu'il s'appelle Septembre Deux Mille Sept.'

JADE

[Folds the top edge of the paper backwards and hands it to DAREKA.] I'd love to meet this guy. Spring 2004. Or at least hear his poetry.

DAREKA

Je voudrais vraiment entendre de nouveau ce poème. [Lays the corpse on the table to read JADE's last line. Looks back to JADE, surprised.] In French? Wow. I am impressed.

JADE

Oui. Nous sommes en France, et le cadavre exquis est un chose français, n'est-ce pas?

DAREKA

It is good. I'm impressed.

LUCILE

I have it! Spring 2004's poem. He mailed it to me written on the back of a child's drawing. [She places the nub of the joint on the ashtray and exits.]

DAREKA

[Folds the top of the paper back and hands it to ADELAIDE. For the rest of the scene, the corpse moves around the circle counterclockwise, each poet writing two lines and folding the paper back so only one line is visible before passing it on.] Adé? You are next?

LUCILE

[Reenters holding a large piece of paper with a colorful, crude finger-painting on its back.] Voici le texte. Ecoutez.

As LUCILE reads Printemps Deux Mille Quatre's poem, stage lights fade. A spotlight appears center stage. JADE rises and walks into it. LUCILE's voice continues to be heard, softly, as JADE speaks.

JADE

Holy fuck. I wish my fourteen-year-old self could see this. She wouldn't believe it and at the same time would be completely unsurprised. I'm in France to perform poetry. I'm sitting in a hash-smoke-filled parlor writing an exquisite corpse with three beautiful French poets at 3AM. This is it. I am now the thing I always wanted to be.

AUDIENCE

Art thou not still imitating?

JADE

Yes, sure. But that's part of why humans invented recorded language in the first place, isn't it? So they could pass down archetypes and ways of being so other people would be able to see and learn a lot of different ways of being without having to figure them all out themselves.

AUDIENCE

Dost thou not wish to be at all original?

JADE

I don't know if that's possible. There's too much information everywhere. Everyone's too aware of what's come before.

AUDIENCE

Dost thou believest we exist? Doth thou believest we art watching thee right now?

JADE

I honestly don't know. Not really. At least not literally. But I feel like there's something inside of me or outside of me that's witnessing all of this, and I have felt that since I've had an idea of myself at all. It's probably the way I was raised. I was introduced to most life situations through sitcoms with studio audiences and old movies and books. My role models were all celebrities I knew through paparazzi and editorials, or they were fictional characters. I was the God-eye watching their stories. Then as I got older, God became flesh, and I started living the stories myself, but life, to me, was still a story to be witnessed.

AUDIENCE

What wantest thou?

JADE

What do you mean?

AUDIENCE

Why doeth any of this? Wherefore dost thou not just sitteth at home watching television and livest through the stories of others as all of thy high school friends art content to do?

JADE

I guess I'm fucked up.

AUDIENCE

Thou art not fucked-up. Nor art thou special. Thou art just like everyone else. Now, telleth us, what wantest thou?

JADE

To connect with people. Like I'm doing now with you. To be fully human and have people see me be human and see their own humanity by seeing me see mine.

AUDIENCE

And thou believest thou art by traipsing through France reading poetry?

JADE

I don't know, but this feels more like that than anything else I've done in my whole life.

AUDIENCE

Wherefore?

JADE

Because in art we see ourselves in others. Because art can't exist in a vacuum. It needs at least one viewer. As soon as you add in another person, the art changes. It becomes part the artist, part the other person.

It's like le cadavre exquis. We only see part of what the last artist intended. The rest is all our own extrapolation. Then it keeps going and going until it's alive on its own, without any of us. It's like sex. Or love. It exists between two people and is the relationship between two people, but it also becomes its own thing that's bigger and more universal than either or both of them. When you create something with another artist or with an audience, that's procreation. That's childbirth.

AUDIENCE

Stop fingerfucking thyself and telleth us what thou wantest.

JADE

To feel like I matter. Like all of it matters. To feel like somebody sees me and understands. To feel like it's not just some cold, mechanical accident that I was born, that I can say words with my mouth, that I see other people with my eyes, or that I touch them with my hands and skin.

AUDIENCE

Stop trying to be poetic. Say what you mean. What do you want?

JADE

Not to be alone.

House lights fade, as well as all stage lights except for one bright white spotlight on JADE. The spotlight dims steadily for one full minute until the entire house is black.

END SCENE, END ACT I

INTERMISSION

Si la plus petite personne reste chez lui, et ae toutes les fleurs dans le monde se donnent rendez-vous dans son sofa pour se faire un bain de racine en jouant au billard avant de se plonger dans Molière, qui aime tellement ça, célibertin qui se justifie par son art amer, et par les remparts qui l'entourent. Chaque mot le guide en NEWS TIME ou en GARAMON, une caligraphie très simple, comme le point où l'océan touche la plage. Mais quand on choisit d'écrire sur des pétals avec de l'encre en pollen, on n'obtient pas grand'chose mais au moins ça sent bon comme quand, tu croque dans du savon. Ta bouche fait des bulles, et ça te pique la langue, et tu finis par tout recacher. Tu me balances ici ces infamités. Pourqui te prends-tu ? Pourquoi tu es si aggressif ? Calme toi, temporise toi. Le monde n'est pas si mauvais. Toutes les personnes que tu aimes, te t'aiment aussi.

DAREKA   Adélaïde

                                        Jade   male

le 26/01/2012
03:57

Chapter Seventeen
What We Wrote

Le Cadavre

Si la plus petite personne reste chez lui, et avec toutes les fleurs dans le monde on se donne rendez-vous dans son sofa pour se faire un bain de racine en jouant au bridge, avant de se plonger dans Molière, qui aime tellement çà, ce libertin qui se justifie par son art amer, et par les remparts qui l'entourent. Chaque mot le guide en NEWS TIME ou en GARAMON, une calligraphie très simple, comme le point ou l'ocean touche la plage. Mais quand on choisit d'écrire sur des pétales avec de l'encre en pollen, on n'obtient pas grand chose, mais au moins çà sent bon. Comme quand tu croques dans du savon. Ta bouche fait des bulles, et çà te pique la langue, et tu finis par tout recracher. Tu me balances ici ces infamités. Pour qui te prends tu? Pourquoi tu es si aggresifs? Calme toi, temporise toi. Le monde n'est pas si mauvais. Toutes les personnes que tu aimes, t'aiment aussi.

★ ★ ★

The Corpse

(translation)

If the smallest person stays at home by himself, and with all the flowers in the world we rendezvous on his couch for a root bath while playing bridge before diving into Molière, who likes it so much—that libertine justifying himself through his bitter art, and the ramparts around him. Each word guides him in TIMES NEW ROMAN or in GARAMOND, a very simple calligraphy, like the point where the ocean touches the beach. We use pollen ink to write on petals. We never get much, but at least it smells good. When you bite into soap, your mouth foams, your tongue stings, and you end up spitting all of it out. Now you're just throwing infamies. Who do you think you are? Why so aggressive? Slow down, calm yourself. The world isn't so bad. All the people you love love you back.

Chapter Eighteen
Jade is a Jade is a Jade is a Jade

I picked Jade because it meant jade. If I'd picked something like Lennon or Shakespeare that would have been a statement. Elvis Costello did this and it worked for him, but that's because he does what he does. I do what I do and wanted a name that was what it was.

Sylvan was a slant rhyme with Dylan (who was a hero) but it meant what it meant. Jade and Sylvan were both English words for real things. Jade—a rock and a color. Sylvan—something in/of the forest. One noun and one adjective, or maybe two adjectives. In the phonebook (when there were phonebooks), it would be *Sylvan, Jade*, and would mean a rock in/of the forest. In normal American order, individual to family, my name was a green forest. Nothing more or less romantic than that.

But then there's jade—talismans, idols, exotic half-nude beauties in veils, ancient China. There's sylvan—wood elves, saddhus, girls in fairytale rape parables. When I tell people my name or hear it spoken, it still feels heavy and clunky, associations flying everywhere. If I could have chosen a name that meant nothing—without the connotations of Nothing—I would have.

In French, Jade means jade. In the English-speaking United States, the name Jade is uncommon enough to intrigue, but not so uncommon that it takes strangers more than a couple of repetitions to hear it when meeting a Jade. In France, it's one of the names they print on souvenir keychains of pink Tour Eiffels. When I learned how to pronounce it in French (soft *j*, flat *a*, afterthought of *e*, dipthong after hard *d*), I only needed to say it once before people nodded and said Enchanté(e), Jade.

I liked the word queer because it meant unique and started with a *q* (what word starts with *q?*) and felt lighter than bisexual. It didn't have the word "sexual" in it for one thing. It didn't carry a hundred sexy sociopathic film villains in the spaces between its syllables.

When I told my mom I called myself queer, she said in her generation "queer" was like saying "fag." I explained reclamation and she nodded and said, *That's nice. I just won't say it.*

When I told my mom I called myself Jade and that the government now called me Jade, she was quiet, as though I'd rejected a much-pondered Christmas present. It took her a while, but she calls me Jade to my face now. To my dad or my Grandma, she calls me Jen(ny/i) still, but this is for them and not for her. She writes Jade on my Christmas presents. She gives me jade necklaces and earrings.

When I've talked to Caleb about transitioning, he's never said he felt like he was a man "trapped in a woman's body." He just said this body felt more right.

When I was young and called myself Jenny, it didn't feel right. I picked Jade not because it felt right, but because it meant what it meant. When I call myself Jade or someone else calls me Jade, it still doesn't feel right.

When I was with Thade, I called myself Jeni and I mostly called myself queer or bi. Sometimes when we'd go out, he would dress up like a woman, shaved legs and all, and I would dress up like a man, bound chest and all. Sometimes I would sleep with women while we were dating. Sometimes he was okay with this, and sometimes he pretended to be okay. Sometimes during and after I was with Thade I called myself straight just because I'd mostly had relationships with men. When I called myself straight and had sex with women, I felt like a bad person.

When I was with Luke, I called myself Jade and I mostly called myself straight. Luke was tall and played baseball, and when we met, he pursued me like I'd read about guys doing in my friends' issues of Cosmo at middle school slumber parties. He even grilled me a steak. When we went out, he always wore the suit jacket and I always wore the little black dress. For a long time after we broke up, I had sex with both men and women but it was a long time before I called myself queer again. When I started calling myself queer again, I'd still had way more penises against my bare skin than vaginas.

When I called myself queer and had had more penises than vaginas against my skin, I felt like a bad person.

When I've had to write about myself and call myself she or her, it doesn't feel right—in my head I hear a genderless voice, somewhere between and/or outside of she and he and her and him.

When I write about myself in France, I feel like I'm creating a character from nothing. I'm doing it because I have to in order to tell a story. These words are gobs of paint I'm lobbing at some invisible creature, trying to give it form.

Chapter Nineteen
Illuminations

The grey-green winter pasturelands of Eastern France glided past us on the train to Champagne. None of us was fully awake or asleep, but there was a woman in front of me and Julian who appeared to be napping. I blew my nose as quietly as I could.

Our parting with Adélaïde had been hazy and brief. After the corpse the night before, she went back to her apartment and I crawled into bed beside a fetal Caleb. When I woke up, Julian was asleep on the couch in the living room. He woke up smiling and stretched like a languorous cat. Dareka and Lucile wandered out of Lucile's room. Lucile had to go to work, so Adélaïde came back to drive us to our 9:35h train to Champagne. Dareka was going back to Paris on a 9:50h train to audition drummers for his band. He would meet us in Reims that evening for the show. He assured us that someone would pick us up from the station in Champagne. He said we should call him if we had any problems.

He bought us a large bag full of croissants and pains au chocolat before we left, and we sat in the living room of Lucile's apartment quietly drinking instant coffee and eating pastry. We rode to the station in near silence. The sky was still overcast and the air was damp. *Thank you for our tour*, was all I could think to say to Adélaïde as we groggily bisou'd goodbye. Even at this hour, she was wearing her *Casablanca* hat.

Caleb was three rows back on the train propped against the window with a t-shirt covering his face as Julian told me with manic post-hook-up aphasia about he and Scott's many eerie synchronicities. I was sitting by the window. As we talked he looked just past me to his reflection, occasionally shifting his gaze for brief touchstones of eye contact. I wasn't sure if he knew (or cared) if I noticed this or not.

I just feel like I deserve to have a young, beautiful lover, he said. I never had that. I was raised in Virginia where the only other gay kid in my school got beat up in a parking lot and almost killed. I was fucking terrified to be gay, and I wound up being practically celibate from the time I was seventeen till I was twenty-four. That was my sexual peak, and I missed it. I missed out on the entire experience of young romance. I feel completely, utterly cheated.

Yeah, I said. *I feel like I might be too old to really experience romance now too. I feel like you have to, like, believe in stuff to go in for that. You have to believe that someone else can complete you. I remember feeling like that, but I don't feel that way now. I don't think you can ever go back.*

But you've had romance. I mean, you were with Luke.

That's one of the reasons I worry I can't do it anymore. That was romantic, yes, but it was completely fucked up and manipulative and kind of abusive. I realized after that how many stories I told myself to keep myself in it. It scares me to think about what we can get ourselves to do if we can make up a story we believe to support it.

Julian shrugged. *Well, I'm sure you'll find someone. You're beautiful and talented. It's easier for women, anyway. Your sexual peak is later.* He heaved a windy sigh. *Plus, you're bi, so your pool is way wider than mine. You'll be fine. I'm fucked.*

Julian put in his earbuds[33], leaned back, and closed his eyes. I followed suit and nodded off to Patti Smith's voice (shout/sing)ing about (G/g)od, freedom, and being so goddamn young.

We were picked up at the Champagne train station by a tall, bearded man in his mid-to-late thirties named Martin who spoke almost no English.

Nous voudrions aller à la Cathédrale... er... avec Joan D'Arc, I said.

La Cathédrale? said Martin. *Ouais, on peut la visiter.*

He stood there eagerly. I was ruined for tour guides. I could almost hear Adélaïde's smoky voice assuring us the Cathedral would be "inspirating."

Julian wanted to go to the Reims Cathedral because he had a thing for Joan of Arc, but he never really told me much about it. The structure was immense. Mythical. The sculpted scenes and characters over the doorways. The gargoyles and buttresses. The taupe grey of the stone. Caleb took out his camera and began to shoot me and Julian as we gaped beneath it.

Nothing is quiet like a medieval Cathedral is quiet. We were the only people inside, and the hall echoed back to us our steps, breaths, and the clicks of Caleb's camera, each lingering noise underlining the silence. When I blew my nose, the whole cavern vibrated.

Caleb was an atheist. It was one of the first things we'd talked about. He'd been raised Catholic and was almost confirmed. He told me how he remembered trying to picture heaven around that time. How the way his mother would describe it, being the same thing forever and ever, sounded nightmarish to him. When he tried to imagine "forever," he couldn't, not any more than he could imagine "nothingness." This idea of Forever terrified him as much as the idea of annihilation.

---

33. He'd been on a bewildering Mariah Carey kick the entire tour.

He stopped going to church when he was thirteen, but he attended Catholic school through high school. His mother was still Catholic when she died. It was harder for her to accept Caleb's renunciation of Catholicism than his decision to become a man.

He still loved the ritual, the symbol, and the artifacts. He created collages from Catholic imagery and icons and made found art from various Catholic paraphernalia. He photographed priests and churches and especially Catholic gravestones. We had this in common in Bloomington, when I was into William Blake, John Milton, and Catholic mysticism. I had a Mary Magdalene medal I bought from a thrift store in San Francisco that I wore on a leather cord around my neck for three years. I saw Eden/Fall metaphors everywhere. In Boston, I got into yoga and a more Buddhist/Hindu brand of mystical agnosticism. Caleb never stopped collecting Catholic fetishes.

We each lit a candle in front of the Virgin. *These places really do feel holy,* I whispered to Caleb as he photographed the seafoam and silver stained glass. He nodded and kept shooting.

Chapter Twenty
La Chambre du Champagne

J ade! Julian! Welcome! I'm so glad you are here. Dareka bisou'd me and Julian but not Caleb. The whole café was probably not more than three square meters. There was a refrigerator on one side, a large bookshelf on the other, and a small kitchen area with a bar and stools along the back. The front wall of the room was a floor-to-ceiling window, so anything going on inside glowed like a silent film from the street. *They have a bottle of nice champagne for you,* said Dareka. *I lied. I told them, 'These Americans, it is very sad. They have never had champagne,' so they bought you some.*

Sébast, the host of the venue, brought us a chilled bottle and three glasses. Sébast, like Bernard and Martin, was pale with short dark hair and a short, dark beard. Unlike Bernard and Martin, he was shorter than me. An attractive, ponytailed Eastern European man in an apron set out a carafe of white wine and a carafe of red wine on the bar in the back. Then he took out a cutting board and a large chef's knife and began slicing hard sausage and cheese.

Julian, Caleb, and I toasted with our champagne. It tasted like sparkly velvet.

They make their own pâté here, too, said Dareka. *Usually interesting types. Duck and rabbit, things like that. Let one of us know when you are hungry, and we will make sure you get a plate.*

Before long, guests started to arrive. We were introduced to nearly everyone as they walked in, but it was starting to become difficult to remember names and faces. The room filled. People began drinking wine and ordering plates of pâté and cheese. Baskets of baguettes were passed around and ripped apart. A small woman of about sixty sat on a bench with her back to the window and began playing atmospheric accordion music.

Sébast performed a poem to begin the evening, and then other members of the audience began to perform. I leaned over to Dareka and I asked if we could try something different here. I wanted to read a couple of my poems in English then have him read the French translations directly afterward. He agreed, and I gave him one of my chapbooks so he could familiarize himself with the words.

Sébast brought us plates of pâté and cheese with large chunks of bread. Julian and I devoured the pâté while Caleb nibbled on the cheese. I finished my glass of champagne and started on Caleb's barely-touched one. All around us, more poetry, more breath, more words.

After we performed, the air in the room was charged. The crowd moved in immediately around us. Everyone wanted to talk to us, to touch us. They told me how much what I'd written had meant to them. They thanked me for coming to France. I sold ten books in fifteen minutes. One woman said I reminded her of Arthur Rimbaud. Another, of Bob Dylan.

More cheese and baguettes were brought out from the back room. When Julian and I were out of champagne, someone brought us each a glass of wine. A few people began to spout poetry spontaneously, but most of the din was conversation. Eventually, the Eastern European man in the apron locked the front door, and a few people began smoking cigarettes and joints inside[34]. The front window grew too steamed up for Julian to see himself in it. The Eastern European man began to chat me up. He looked and spoke nothing like Adélaïde, and I was stupendously uninterested. Sébast paid Julian and me the one hundred euros he'd promised each of us. He told us how much he appreciated our coming through Reims and seemed to really mean it.

Our host in Reims was Élodie, a pretty, slim blond woman with a preppy style and a nose stud. As soon as we got back to her place, Caleb went to bed on the chaise lounge on the landing. Julian and I stayed up with Élodie, her husband, and Sébast drinking desert wine and talking in broken English and broken French about the psychocultural reasons why Americans are so fat.

Les personnes sont malheureuses, I said, sipping the last of the champagne Élodie had bought for us. *Donc ils mangent et mangent parce-que ils croyent que ce va... fill them up. Vous comprennez? En les Etats Unis, tout le monde sont... empty... vide. Tout le monde sont vide, et on veut... fill up avec quelquechose. Donc, on mange et mange, et on fait du shopping, et on bois et fume. Pas seulement un peu, mais TOUT le viande et TOUT les robes et TOUT le whiskey et TOUT les tabacs. Mais on ne peut pas être... full. On est toujours vide, et ce fait peur.*

When you're talking to someone from another culture, finding common experience has to be much more intentional. When you're talking to someone in your demographic in your neighborhood, it's easy. You assume similar taste for farmer's market arugula or *The Daily Show*. The further removed from superficial similarities you get, the more you have to dig to find common ground. Eventually, it becomes so simple. I want. You want. I love. You love. I'm afraid. You're afraid. Etc.

---

34. It had apparently only recently become illegal in France to smoke indoors, and one of the things I remembered most vividly from my trip in 2006 was the thick smoky air in every single bar and café. The new law was evidently a point of much grumbling among the young, artistic, and beautiful French.

Not having the language to say what you mean makes you realize the difference between meaning and accuracy. You have to get creative, and your meaning has to be more important than your ego. You wind up using either very simple language or elaborate metaphors and images. It's a little like poetry.

After my second glass of dessert wine, I said, *Caleb et moi, nous allons aller à Père Lachaise pour voir la tombe d'Oscar Wilde. Vous savez l'histoire?*

L'histoire d'Oscar Wilde? said Élodie.

Oué, l'histoire d'Oscar Wilde, mais aussi l'histoire de la tombe? Comment dans le… nineteen nineties… beaucoup des personnes a elle embrassé avec rouge à lèvres. Ensuite, le gouvernement a elle nettoyé, et… put up a glass barrier.

Élodie and the two dark-haired men nodded. I continued.

So, the thing is, le chose est, aside from being a huge role model/poster child for gay and queer culture for the past several decades, Oscar Wilde was also a martyr for art, romance, and for romantic art. What most people don't know about his trials—meaning, the trials in which he was accused of being a sodomite, which led to his imprisonment, and which led to his death—what most people don't know about them is that he was given the chance to flee, like, many times. He was a popular guy in London. A toast of the town. No one wanted to see him imprisoned. The authorities, everyone hoped he would go abroad, but he chose to stay. He didn't admit to fucking men, but he publicly made a case for art and aesthetics and a confusing type of love more complex, subtle, and profound than prescribed Victorian courtship or modern so-called romantic comedies. He lost the trials, but his ideology would only lose if he didn't walk his body through the tragedy, and he understood that.

Most gender studies and queer theory-oriented people I know say that the concept of the homosexual started at the moment a court of law decided that Wilde, the aesthete, the poet, was the "type of person" who would commit sodomy. Before that, having sex with someone of the same gender was an act, not an identity.

The thing is, identity was Wilde's best medium, and his masterpiece was his own personality. To be honest, I never cared for Wilde's poetry. I love his letters and essays and enjoy his plays, but his verse was too Victorian for me. The singsong rhyme scheme always seemed clunky, and a lot of his lines are just too cliché, even allowing for the time period.

But Wilde was a poet if anyone has ever been a poet. His life was poetry and he lived poetry. He wrote about how he lived poetry, and referred to himself as a poet in his writing. The personality that he worked so hard to excavate from the silt of Victorian society and express to the full extent of its individuality was The Poet[35], as it had to be contextualized in his specific time and place.

When he was released finally, he fled London alone and in disgrace. In France, he wrote "The Ballad of Reading Gaol," about his experience in prison. He repeats again and again the line, 'Each man kills the thing he loves[36].'

Oscar Wilde died exiled. He wasn't buried in Père Lachaise. He was buried in some random graveyard outside the Parisian city limits. He wasn't moved to where he is now until years later. That was when they built the big monument.

He died for art. He died for beauty. He died for love. He died... I trailed off.

Julian was horizontal and three-quarters-asleep clutching a pillow on his futon. I scanned the other faces in the room and could see most of my English was lost on Sébast, Élodie, and her husband. They nodded and fingered their glasses in a polite, sleepy show of attentiveness.

I switched back to French feebly and tried to start a conversation about gay marriage legislation in France versus the U.S. Everyone was tired. I kept calling Élodie "vous," and she corrected me and told me I should be using "tu," since she was only a couple years older than me. That didn't seem right. She was married with two daughters and a real

---

35. I was reading *De Profundis* at the time, which I'd downloaded on the iPad a friend and patron had given me before this tour.

36. The final stanza, which I didn't know at the time, is *And all men kill the thing they love,/ By all let this be heard,/ Some do it with a bitter look,/ Some with a flattering word,/ The coward does it with a kiss,/ The brave man with a sword!*

career. I was still living in a room lit with Christmas lights and writing poems on my bed like a college student.

Julian interrupted Sébast mid-sentence by started to snore. I yawned. My vision was getting hazy.

Je dois me coucher, I said. *Merci pour le vin et le conversation. Je suis trés fatiguée maintenant. Merci. Bonne nuit.*

I downed a full glass of water and curled up on the stiff cot. My heart was racing, and I knew I would be at least a little hungover the next morning. My left leg was cramped along the outside, ankle to knee to hip. I thought, as I often did, that I wish I'd started all of this younger. If I were twenty-one, instead of twenty-nine, the couch-crashing and the strange-town hangovers would seem much more romantic. Now, I could feel my body beginning to protest. My joints were at the brink of growing stiff and brittle.

For a moment, I wished for a familiar, soft bed, with my own lamp and glass on the end table, a tired routine to wake up to, and partner so familiar I could be annoyed by their sleep-breathing and/ or their stealing the covers. I thought of Thade and our apartment in Bloomington, how I could have had one bed with one person my whole life. But I couldn't do it, just as I could never hold a regular job for more than a few months at a time. No matter how much I convinced myself I wanted these things, my body rejected them like bad grafts. No ordinary life seemed worth living to me. Again and again, my choice was clear: either I kill myself, or I go for the impossible thing. There was nothing to lose, and I was curious about the stories of my idols. They'd had bodies, just like me. I had to know if it was possible to step my flesh into the mythical realm of poets and gods.

Once, in Bloomington, I'd asked a fifty-something interfaith minister about his conception of the self/soul as it related to our choices. *Say I'm trying to decide if I should throw my empty water bottle in the recycling bin or leave it on the sidewalk for someone else to clean up. Am I looking for something that pre-exists inside of me to tell me what to do, or is it my choice that makes me into the type of person who would do that thing?*

He paused for about ten seconds, then said, carefully, that some people believe in the soul and some people don't, but either way, most of us can agree that we exist and experience something inside or around us that we label "self," and that it doesn't matter if our selves are created through our choices or our choices are emanations of our selves. Either way (or both ways), we are what we choose to be.

Then he said, *You better make the choice you're willing to die for because we all die for what we do.*

Chapter Twenty-One
The Poem I Performed in Reims and Louis Remembered from the Cantab

Plates

There is a frigidity that does not wait for bonfires and Eastern Standard Time to wiggle into living bones. Dopplegangers linger terrifying and invisible, they shadow our every move, watch like voyeurs through bushes at our hushed conversations on futons after the kids are in bed—as you Google German sopranos and try on new shoes, your other life is always wrapped around you, a film of ether in the most floral parts of the brain. One step left or right and you could have been a cowboy, a screen actor, a witch, a freemason. Somewhere your hands are filthy with dirt from your mango farm, your pro tennis career, the dig site where you discovered a new species of dinosaur.

Demons only demonize, I tell myself. If they are so smart, why aren't they standing here in a matter suit, like me, drinking wine and baking cakes, kissing and being kissed. No one kisses demons. They don't even have lips of their own.

★ ★ ★

My roommate is eating an apple. I hate her mouth for how it snaps off the flesh in wet tears, hate the smack of her tonguing the fruit, the oblivious way she licks her lips, the way she eats all day and does not gain weight, but I love her because she has a mouth to eat and speak with, because she is human and wants and is fulfilled. It is a wobbly tightrope.

I try to concentrate describe something someone uneducated might call the soul. I am staccatoed by my neighbor lobbing limp beanbags at a slab of particle board. They fly like winsome empanadas flung from a catapult, land with thwaps. I do not know his name but he wears a fitted navy baseball cap backwards on his skull.

★　★　★

I want to love this place how monks talk of washing dishes—what once clean, now dirty, now clean—there is a cycle to everything, not linear like breaking plates. I do everything too quickly. My plates are always breaking.

I want to love the plates, want to wipe the flotsam slurry from their faces hard with glaze chanting om mane padme hum, want to clean them, dirty them, clean them again.

I made up my own Lord's Prayer last week before scraping off my monkey fur with razorblades and heading out to the bar. I found the Body of God in day old bread the bakery leaves out on the curb for the bums. I never felt so hungry.

I want to go on vacation with my body and leave my mind at home to bury herself in algorithms and iambs.

I would seek out sensation anywhere I could, open my legs to the Mayor of Allston City and his denizens of beer bottle stab wounds, to the priest in Galway who lingered too long dropping God's body on my pink flower tongue, to the teenagers by the bridge at the canal, Dr. Pepper bottles brimming with SoCo, to the old folks in their eponymous homes, to the sad aging swingers swapping bruised husband for bruised wife.

The inside of me is filled with broken plates. Have your way with me. Compared to you all I am six times a virgin. Let's get right down to it. You cannot love in a straight line without breaking. There is no way back home.

★ ★ ★

I am not a singer, a poet, or an especially good friend. I prefer to be naked. All words are just clothes and they itch like thriftstore synthetics. Let me lie here in the dirt and let the sky cover me like heat, like milk. Paint me if you like, I will not notice. Bring your mouth to the crux of my thighs and drink the blood which is the origin of all life as I dream of sky burials, of the monks that hold the cubed human flesh out to the birds who clean the bones delicate as fine plates. Those birds were dinosaurs once, those monks were monkeys, and all of us used to be stars. Let us dine together. I have set the table. There is a place for everyone.

★ ★ ★

Assiettes
(traduction)

Il existe une certaine frigidité qui n'attend ni les feux de joie ni l'heure américaine pour s'immiscer en frétillant à l'intérieur d'os pleins de vie.

Des sosies s'attardent terrifiants et invisibles, ils prennent en filature chacun de nos gestes espionnent comme des voyeurs à travers les buissons nos conversations etouffées sur des futons nocturnes après que les enfants sont couchés—lorsque vous googlez les sopranos allemandes et essayez de nouvelles chaussures, votre autre vie est toujours enveloppée autour de vous, un film d'éther dans les parties les plus fleuries de votre cerveau. Un pas à gauche ou à droite et vous auriez pu être un cow-boy, un acteur de cinéma, une sorcière, un franc-maçon. Vos mains par endroit sont salies par la terre de votre ferme de mangues, votre carrière de tennis pro, le site de fouilles où vous avez découvert une nouvelle espèce de dinosaures.

Je me dis que les démons ne font que démoniser. s'ils sont si intelligents, pourquoi ne sont-ils pas ici dans un costume matériel, comme moi, à boire du vin et faire des gâteaux, embrasser et être embrassé. Personne n'embrasse les démons. Ils n'ont même pas de lèvres.

★   ★   ★

Ma colocataire est en train de manger une pomme. Je déteste sa bouche et la façon dont elle s'arrache avec un bruit sec à la chair hespéridée en larmes humides, je déteste le claquement de ses coups de langue sur le fruit, la manière oublieuse dont elle se lèche les lèvres, la façon dont elle mange tous les jours et ne prend pas de poids, mais je l'aime parce qu'elle a une bouche pour manger et parler avec, parce qu'elle est humaine et désire et s'accomplit. C'est une corde raide bien flageolante.

J'essaye de me concentrer, de décrire quelque chose quelqu'un d'inculte pourrait appeler l'âme. Je suis interrompue en staccato par mon voisin et ses poufs mous jetés en l'air contre un panneau de particules. Ils s'envolent comme de séduisantes empanadas lancées d'une catapulte, et atterrissent comme des gifles. Je ne sais pas son nom mais il porte une casquette de baseball bleu marine, vissée à l'envers sur son crâne.

★ ★ ★

Je veux aimer cet endroit comme les moines s'entretiennent de lavage de vaisselle, de ce qui fut propre, puis sale, et propre à nouveau. Il y a un cycle pour tout, ce n'est pas linéaire comme casser des assiettes. Je fais tout trop vite. Mes assiettes se brisent tout le temps.

Je veux aimer les assiettes, je veux essuyer la gadoue naufragée sur leurs visages durs comme de l'émail en chantant om mane padme hum. Je veux les nettoyer, les salir, les nettoyer à nouveau.

J'ai inventé mon propre Notre Père la semaine dernière avant de racler ma fourrure de singe avec des lames de rasoir et avant de sortir pour le bar. J'ai trouvé le corps de Dieu dans le pain d'hier que la boulangerie avait sorti sur le trottoir pour les clochards. Je n'ai jamais eu autant faim.

Je veux aller en vacances avec mon corps et laisser mon esprit à la maison à s'enterrer dans des algorithmes et des vers iambiques.

Je rechercherais le sensationnel partout où je le pourrais, j'ouvrirais mes jambes pour le maire de la ville d'Allston et ses habitants lacérés à coup de bouteille de bière, au prêtre de Galway, qui prenait trop de temps pour déposer le corps de Dieu sur ma langue fleur rose, aux adolescents près du pont sur le canal, et leurs canettes de soda pleines de bourbon trop sucré, aux vieux dans leurs maisons éponymes, aux tristes échangistes vieillissants qui échangent mari meurtri contre femme meurtrie.

L'intérieur de moi est rempli d'assiettes cassées. Faites de moi ce que vous voulez. En comparaison de vous tous je suis six fois vierge.

Passons aux choses sérieuses. Vous ne pouvez aimer en ligne droite sans rompre. Il n'y a pas de chemin de retour.

★   ★   ★

Je ne suis pas une chanteuse, un poète ou une particulièrement bonne amie. Je préfère être nue. Les mots ne sont que des vêtements et ils démangent comme des fibres synthétiques glanées aux puces. Laissez-moi étendue là dans la crasse et laissez le ciel me couvrir comme la chaleur, comme du lait. Badigeonnez-moi de peinture si vous voulez, je ne remarquerai même pas. Posez votre bouche à la croisée de mes cuisses et buvez le sang qui est l'origine de toute vie alors que je rêve de funérailles célestes, pour les moines qui distribuent la chair humaine en cubes aux oiseaux qui nettoient des os aussi délicats que des assiettes fines. Ces oiseaux furent un temps des dinosaures, ces moines furent des singes, et nous étions tous des étoiles. Dinons ensemble, voulez-vous. J'ai mis la table. Il y a une place pour chacun.

Chapter Twenty-Two
Gertrude Stein

*D*areka's apartment was up the hill from the Belleville Metro stop on the Right Bank. He shared it with another artist, a thirty-two-year-old musician (male, pale, with a dark beard) and a twenty-three year old American graduate student (female, short, Jewish), and it was about as nice and clean as you would expect. The only two remarkable particulars about the place were the view from Dareka's room, where, he showed us, if you climbed out the window and stood on the very edge of the fire escape, you could glimpse, just over the rooftops of the surrounding cityscape, the corona of the Tour Eiffel[37], and the fact that it was about a ten-minute walk to Père Lachaise.

Julian spread out on the pull-out couch in the living room to take a nap. Caleb and I slumped at the large dining room table, staring into space for about five minutes. Then Caleb said,

Do you want to go now?

I paused, then sighed. I didn't look at him.

---

37. This view, he told us with a grin, had led to many a first kiss with many a young lady.

I'm just worried we won't be back again, said Caleb. *I mean, aren't we supposed to stay with someone else the rest of the time in Paris?*

Yeah, tomorrow we're staying with Dareka's band-mate. Some woman who's name I forget.

Do you know where she lives?

No idea.

We should go now.

I know.

We walked up the winding, hilly streets to the somber stone wall that surrounded Père Lachaise. The entrance closest to Dareka's apartment was the farthest away from Oscar Wilde, but was the closest to Gertrude Stein, whose grave I'd never seen. When we walked in, a groundskeeper and a guard were talking by some sort of official-looking shed about three meters away from us. The groundskeeper was leaning half of his body on a shovel[38]. One of them said something to us that I didn't understand.

Quoi? I asked. He repeated it, but I was too flustered by the interruption to separate the words into meaning.

He said it's closing in less than an hour, said Caleb.

I thanked the groundskeeper and asked him if he knew where Gertrude Stein was. The way he pronounced *Gertrude Stein,* I wouldn't have understood him unless I already knew what he was saying. He told us the section number and pointed us toward it. The guard also handed us folded tourist's map.

It was farther from the entrance than it looked on the map. We walked past block after block of sectioned-off gravestones and ornate, temple-like monuments. One section was a dedicated Holocaust memorial, its centerpiece an eerie expressionist sculpture—a twisted bronze conflagration of writhing ghosts.

---

38. This detail may be an apocrypha of memory.

The section the groundskeeper named was a large grey square of land rowed with rather anomalously plain grave markers, all dull grey or glossy black. Gertrude Stein was not indicated on the map, so we had no choice but to walk up and down every row of gravestones and read each names.

Row after row, she wasn't there. Sometimes, as we made our way down a line I would spy a heavily-decorated grave a few meters away and conjecture that that must be it, but it never was. Some of the graves were so covered in flowers I had to move them to read the names. Most of the adorned names had been dead at least several decades, but I didn't recognize any of them as famous. When I moved the flowers, even just to read the names, I felt weird about it. I always put them back.

As we started to make it closer to one edge abutting the stone wall of the cemetery, the graves began trading their French for Hebrew and their crosses for stars of David.

As we walked down the last row on the very edge along the pathway, we saw a large stone-framed bed of stones. The stones were sized from grape to golf ball. There were hundreds, maybe thousands, all filling this vast rectangular stone bed. There was nothing remarkable about the stones other than their placement and company. They all were just stones you could find anywhere on the ground on the cemetery. The headstone also was stacked with these stones, as if the stones were water and could flow off the headstone into the stone bed. The stones were all grey as the sky or black as closed eyes. The headstone was wide, clean, and geometric, with only the words GERTRUDE STEIN carved on its front and only the words ALICE B. TOKLAS carved on its back.

I stood looking across the large stone bed at her name. I probably said something in my head to her, whatever she now was. Something very heartfelt, I'm sure, and very unoriginal. From the other side of the headstone, Caleb took a picture of me looking.

I walked around to the back of the headstone alongside Caleb. The letters were sharp and deep, and I knelt and touched them.

When I stood up, I saw, placed at the very apex of the pile of stones on the headstone, one rock that was not black or grey, but deep burgundy red. It was shaped like a heart[39].

I don't know what I should leave, I said.

Do you want to leave a rock? said Caleb.

No, it doesn't feel sincere. It wouldn't mean anything to me.

Well, what else do you have? Or we could walk around a little bit and find something maybe.

I kind of want to take a rock.

Okay.

Is that terrible? Is that wrong?

Caleb shrugged. *I don't think anything's wrong if you do it for the right reasons.*

It feels right. I want to take a rock with me. I'll put it on my altar at home.

Okay. Then take a rock then.

I reached out and lifted the heart-shaped rock reverently off its cradle. If anything ever feels right, it felt right.

What in God's name do you think you're doing? said a nasal, Irish-accented voice.

I looked over the headstone to see a slim, frail, white-haired man wearing a sweater vest and a backpack. He was holding his smart phone horizontally aimed at the grave, apparently halted in the process of taking a picture.

---

39. Valentine, not anatomical.

I walked around the grave to stand near the man, and Caleb followed. I showed the man the rock. *I was going to take this because I always leave things at graves, but here, it felt right to take something home. Is that wrong?*

The man wouldn't make eye-contact, he just shook. *How can you even ask that? Is it wrong?*

I evened out my voice. *I'm sorry. I'll put it back. I've never heard anything about taking something from a grave if it's sacred to you.*

Go ahead. Play the ugly American. He shook his head making grunting noises of disgust.

I mean, doesn't the staff clean it all up eventually anyway? I said. *If people for the past eighty years have been leaving stones here, I'm pretty sure it would be more than overflowing by now, unless it's been cleared out a few times.*

God! He made more grunting noises and squinted at me out of the corner of his eye. *Fine, take it,* he said. He held up his smart phone and took two more pictures, previewing them both before glancing at me one more time with unmitigated disdain and walking away from us down the path.

I looked at Caleb[40]. He shrugged. I pocketed the rock.

Through the clouds we could see that the sun was low in the sky. Père Lachaise would be closing soon, and Wilde's grave was on the opposite edge. We navigated as quickly as we could, Caleb with his short legs and me with my worsening limp, along uphill paths threaded through monuments and mausoleums. The markers were more frequently in the rococo style nearer to the center. They gradually became more modest as we climbed away from it. We were both out of breath. The sun was setting, and the wind was cold when we finally got there.

---

40. As long as we've been friends, whenever Caleb and I go places together, it seems like I'm always getting yelled at by someone for doing something I oughtn't. Caleb hates getting yelled at, and so rarely does things he's afraid he oughtn't. One of the reasons he mostly shoots self-portraits and portraits of me, in fact, is because he hates asking permission and hates being reprimanded for not asking permission.

The grave was immaculate and encased by four unceremonious glass walls. The stone angel[41] swept along its place[42] clean and unperverted[43]. For a moment, panting, we both just stood there. Kisses of desperate saliva and lipstick smeared across the glass like children's car-window mouth-prints. Someone had written, *Oscar, je t'aime,* in red lipstick across the lower left of the barrier's face.

A young blond couple walked up behind us carrying the same map the guard had given me. They spoke to each other in German, looking at the map and pointing at the grave in turn. Then the girl stepped forward and stood smiling in front of the glass while the guy took a smart phone picture. The guy said something in German and the girl said something back and then she turned around and kissed the glass while the guy repositioned himself and took some more pictures. Caleb and I stepped backward a few paces to get out of the shot. The wind stung my face and made my fingers go numb. I wished I'd brought gloves.

When the German couple stepped away to huddle together and view the pictures, I looked at Caleb. He'd taken his camera out of its case and stood there with it half-poised.

I guess I should kiss it, I said.

Okay.

Right? I mean, that's the only thing I can really do.

Sure. It's up to you.

I took a step forward. *Crap. I don't have any lipstick.*

---

41. Gertrude Stein and Alice B. Toklas were acquaintances of Jacob Epstein and saw him when he came to Paris to place his angel on Oscar Wilde's grave.

42. I noticed that Louis had paraphrased the line he told me was Wilde's epitaph.

43. Epstein's angel originally included a penis, which was so badly vandalized it was removed.

I remembered packing and holding lipstick in my hand and choosing not to put it in. I remembered thinking I didn't wear lipstick anymore, that lipstick, along with Chanel perfume and skin-tight mini-dresses, were things I wore when I was dating Luke. I then remembered remembering the Wilde grave-kissing plan and remembered thinking I'd buy lipstick in Paris if I needed it. I hadn't bought any, and here we were. Without lipstick, the kiss would be useless.

Before we could figure out another plan, we heard the anemic honk of a golf cart horn. A guard had pulled up behind us to let us know Père Lachaise was closing. The German tourists linked arms and walked toward the nearest exit. Caleb immediately shoved his camera into its bag.

We should go, he said.

Yeah, I know.

Maybe we can come back another time. We can find some lipstick somewhere.

Sure. Maybe.

The golf cart honked again. Caleb and I followed after the German couple. I was hobbling. Every other step hurt.

Chapter Twenty-Three
La Fée Verte

It was Julian's and my last show together before he left for Germany and then Denmark. The gig was in a tiny stone, dungeon-esque basement of a yuppie nightclub in Oberkampf. I wore a collared shirt with a skinny tie tied in a four-in-hand knot, black pants, and a vest. The humidity had curled my hair to tight, wild ringlets[44]. There were about twelve audience members. I sold three books and bought one drink and came away twenty euro in the black.

After the show, we were all milling around outside the club as the city's night chasers started to emerge from their glittered and perfumed burrows to grab their street crêpes pregnant with Nutella et coco et banane and get on their collective and respective drinks/dances/smokes.

So what's the plan? said Julian, running his fingers through his hair and eyeing the clubgoers that slid past like quicksilver. Caleb and I shrugged.

---

44. Later, when a Dylan-obsessed friend saw the photos Caleb took from this evening, she made several rapid succession *Don't Look Back* jokes.

Dareka materialized out of the din of the bar. He put one hand on my shoulder and one hand on Julian's shoulder. *Guys, do you want to go to a bar with thirty different types of absinthe?* he said[45].

I was absolutely exhausted, and Caleb looked like he was wilting around the weight of his camera, but it was Friday night and we were in Paris. I looked at Julian. He smiled and raised his eyebrows.

Sure, I said. *Is it close?*

Yes. It is on the way back to my place.

The bar was a bar. It was dark and decorated with skeleton paraphernalia, oddly colored boudoir-esque lights, and a murder of pale, glammed-out goth kids in various states of lithe shirtlessness writhing around a makeshift dance floor in the back room's backmost corner. The bar itself in the front room was stocked with bottles and bottles of green, white, and blue absinthe. When I walked up, the bartender handed me a menu.

I'd had absinthe about eight times, all of which were when I was under twenty-five. Six of these times involved lighting a sugar cube on fire, five involved Dawn, and three involved me blacking out, vomiting out of other people's cars, and time-traveling to some sweaty, unfamiliar bed, still wearing my clothes from the night before.

But it was Paris on a Friday night, and I was a poet, so I was going to have a glass of absinthe. It was organized like a microbrewery's beer menu. There were columns for price, alcohol content, and wormwood content, along with descriptions of the absinthe's character that I could halfway decipher. I was too tired to care about choosing.

Dareka's American roommate Maureen had joined us after our gig, and she walked up next to me and asked to share the menu, scrunching up her nose like a bunny.

Hey, can you pick something for me? I said.

---

45. Incidentally, Dareka did not drink alcohol at all, or do any drugs. At bars he ordered Coca-Cola, which came in 330ml woman-shaped glass bottles.

Sure! she said. She smiled and her shoulders shrugged up toward her ears. *What are you looking for?*

Something not expensive and not terrible.

She laughed. *Okay! Fair enough.* She took the menu and began to study it.

She was wearing a baggy granny-chic cardigan, a flapper-style frock, and large plastic glasses. Even when she put down the menu, the oversized cardigan forced her to keep her arms bent at the elbow as if she were carrying a shawl.

She ordered for both of us, and we watched as the bartender poured the drinks and placed a small silver spoon over the rim of each one, topped with a sugar cube. He then placed both glasses under its own stream of water flowing from a large glass canister with multiple spigots radiating from its basin like the legs of an octopus. I wasn't sure which was more hypnotic: the thin, gentle stream of clear water cascading over the sugar and diffusing into the cloudy green liquid below or the gradual erosion of the cube as it dissolved under its flow.

When the small ritual was complete, we each took our glasses and carried them back to the room with the dance floor. There, Julian was listening to Dareka describe, amongst highly animated hand gestures, the controversial schism that had recently occurred in Paris between the Grand Slam National and the Coupe de La Ligue Slam de France. Dareka was expressing a less than favorable opinion about the founder and organizer of the former. He gripped his small bottle of Coca-Cola tightly in his left hand.

Caleb was hovering in the corner behind them and in front of an open casket mounted to the wall that displayed a plastic human skeleton. I walked over to him, and we stood with our backs to the corner watching the patrons of the bar.

There were dozens of beautiful young people wearing faerie wings or vinyl skirts or nipple-shielding electrical tape Xs in lieu of shirts.

About half the bar wore some form of fishnet somewhere on their body.

I sipped my absinthe[46]. The intense flavor of licorice woke me up a little, but the alcohol was soporific. I looked at Caleb. We didn't need to say it. He was thirty and I was one year shy of it, and we were both feeling our age.

You know, ten years ago I would have thought this was the coolest thing in the world. I loved bars. I thought facts of the bar—the dim lights, the drinking, the grasping at connectedness through all this obfuscation of the senses, all of this— were so romantic. Now I just look around and see all these people, and I feel like I already know them. That blond girl over there in the sequins? I would have such a crush on her. We'd have a two-week-long romance where she'd overtake my life and crash my car and probably get me fired from some job. Then she'd steal my favorite t-shirt and end up dating some asshole guy with a Poli Sci degree and a big dick. That guy with the blazer and the scarf? We'd hang out for a few months sharing our favorite anime series and talking about Meister Eckhart and Kierkegaard. He'd have a girlfriend who didn't understand him but who he couldn't leave. He'd say how much he wished things were different. He'd tell me that I'm talented and brilliant, and that he'd be very lucky to be with me, but he just couldn't do it.

I swear, said Caleb, *if I hadn't met Leyna, I'd just be alone forever. I'd never date. I'd never talk to people. I'd just hide in my room and make art.*

Yeah. Maybe that's what I should do.

We stood there for a few minutes as silent observers. I experimented shifting my weight in my cowboy boots, trying to find some manner of standing that caused the least amount of pain in my left leg. I started to watch the interaction right in front of us. Maureen had joined Dareka and Julian. She was smiling behind her large glasses and clutching

---

46. I had been trying to cut down on my drinking for about a year. By "trying to," I might mean, "thinking about." Sometimes, while drinking, I talked about quitting drinking entirely. It wasn't good for a body, and I didn't want to go out like Kerouac after all. When I mentioned this intention to Louis, he expressed his disapproval. *It's not that I like drinking*, he said, drinking. *I belieeeeeeve in drinking.* Eye flash. Grin.

her glass of absinthe in her left hand while she used her right hand to gesture. Both elbows remained bent, the oversized shawl draping around them. When she was finished gesturing, her right hand would rejoin the left to lightly finger the glass.

I looked at Caleb. He was watching Maureen, too. I said, *Isn't it interesting how what clothes people wear affects the way they move their bodies?* He locked eyes with me. I said, *I mean, if I were standing here in a short dress instead of pants and a tie, I'd carry myself completely differently. I'd almost feel like a completely different person.*

He smiled, and, for a moment, there was no place where he ended and I began or I ended and he began. *That was the point of* Other People's Clothes, he said. *I noticed how even just the way clothes are cut sort of forces a body into moving a certain way. Something as simple as the difference between a tight tweed skirt constricting your movement and a pair of Levis and a t-shirt. It's like a self-fulfilling prophecy. The clothes are designed for a type of person. Then they sort of bridle the person's flesh into being that type.*

Maureen tossed her head back and opened her mouth wide to mime laughter. I remembered Adélaïde tearing through the moodily lit Dijon streets in her fedora and trench coat. Her laugh sounded like a fox's bark. I sipped my absinthe and found the bottom of the glass. It had disappeared without my noticing.

I think the reason I can't seem to date right is I don't have any sense of a definable linear identity[47], I said. *As far as I'm concerned, there is no me, just a bunch of costumes I try on and get bored with. By the time anyone starts to like anything about my personality, it changes. I become someone else. People fall in love with each other for their personalities. To be loved, you need to believe in your own personality. You need to think you know who you are.*

---

47. When I'd said this to Louis, he'd said, *Well, that's some philosophical garbage. That all sounds rhetorically enlightened and all, but the reality is, you have a Self. You know that.*

Chapter Twenty-Four
The Truth of Masks

I t was raining in Oberkampf. Caleb and I huddled underneath a tiny awning waiting for Agnès to come down and let us in.

Julian had left early that morning after he and I'd shared a restless night's sleep on a sagging queen-sized pull-out couch. He woke me and Caleb (who'd slept on the loveseat a few feet away) by fumbling around the room at 6:50h, packing up his things to catch his 8:14h train. When he said, in a small, authentic voice, *Goodbye, Jade. It was great sharing a tour with you*, my response was an unfortunately cranky, *Thanks. Bye.*

Agnès looked like a bird. She was tall and lanky, with straw-straight dirty-blond hair pulled back in a ponytail. She owned an art gallery in town, and her apartment was full of African masks and carvings. Her left eye was lazy and pointed down and to the left as she made intense eye-contact with her right eye and complained to us about being in a band with Dareka.

If tomorrow's practice goes like rehearsal did on Thursday, I'm out, she said.

It was rough? I said, as Caleb and I removed our soggy shoes, socks, and jackets in her entryway.

She set her bag down dramatically beside two large African drums, pausing with a hand on her hip, gazing away from us out the large sliding glass doors that led to a small cement balcony. *Let's just say he doesn't listen.*

She was white, which I mention because she was from Ghana. She played African drums in Dareka's band. French was her first language, but it was Ghanaian French. She said nobody could understand her accent. When she spoke French people assumed she was English, and when she spoke English, people assumed she was German. She spoke to us in English. When I looked at her and listened to her speak English, she sounded German, but when I closed my eyes she sounded African.

I meet black people in France who tell me I don't have the right to play the drums or to call myself African, she said. She looked at us with her right eye. *I look straight at them and say, 'Ha! I am more black than you are. You don't know anything about Africa. You've never even been outside of Paris. I can hear it in the way you speak.'*

Caleb and I exchanged glances. The way many white people in Europe[48] talked about race made both of us uncomfortable.

She sank into the sofa, then shifted and pressed her hand into the fabric beneath her. *Oh shit,* she said. *It's fucking wet.*

A snow-white Persian cat padded out of the bathroom. Agnès stared at it and held out her wet hand.

I adopted her from a shelter four months ago. This problem only started last month though. I brought her to the vet, and they said there's nothing wrong with her. I don't know. If this keeps up I can't keep her, but I know if I bring her back

---

48. In Amsterdam, before Caleb joined us, Julian and I had spent an evening drinking Grolsch and eating sausages and potatoes in a pot-smoke-filled living room where our three white Dutch hosts repeatedly said the N word just to watch the two Americans jump and blanche

like this they'll kill her. In short, I don't know what to do. She walked past us into the kitchen to wash the cat pee off her hand. *You're not allergic to cats, are you?*

I am, I said. *But I'm allergic to everything. I'm used to it.*

She walked back out to the living room drying her hands with a paper towel. *Well, she's not allowed in your room, anyway.* She opened a door off the living room to a small, windowless guest room with a fully-made queen-sized bed. *How long are you in Paris?* she asked.

Till Tuesday, I said.

Are you staying here?

Caleb and I looked at one another, then back at her. *We're not sure,* said Caleb. *Dareka said something about another one of his bandmates maybe having room for us, didn't he?*

She waved a hand at us and walked back into her kitchen. *Don't be silly. Just stay here. One of the reasons I pay for this stupid apartment is so I can host artists who come through town.* Caleb and I both said thank you.

We unloaded our bags in the guest room. Agnès had to go to work, but she gave us both towels and washcloths and we took turns taking long, hot showers, me first, then Caleb.

I had to take a paint roller and pan out of the bathtub before I got in to shower. I felt like I stayed in there for an hour, but it was really only about ten minutes. When I came out of the bathroom, Caleb was in the kitchen taking pictures out the window. There, over the rooftops of the surrounding buildings, rose the steeple of a Gothic church.

Every window in France has a church, I said.

Apparently, he said.

Caleb went to take a shower, and I went back to the guest room and dropped my towel. I looked at my body in the mirror that hung on the back of the door as I blew my nose on a torn piece of paper towel.

I was not old and I was not young. I was not unattractive and I was not exceptionally beautiful. My breasts sagged a little. My calves were strong and taut. I had feminine hips and thighs and masculine arms and shoulders. My hands were perfectly androgynous.

There are so many stimuli coming at us every second, and we have to figure out some way[49] to organize it all. The details we notice become our experience, our experience becomes our story, and our story becomes who we are.

I don't know how to tell if I'm a poet because I notice poetic things or if I notice poetic things because I'm a poet. I am a poet, so I notice poetic things. I notice poetic things, so I am a poet. If I weren't a poet, I don't know what I'd be.

It took me years to tell people I was a poet. When I was younger I was afraid they'd laugh and say something like, *That doesn't make you special. Everyone's a poet.*

I tell people I'm a poet now all the time, and no one's ever said that to me. If they said that to me now, I don't think I'd think they were wrong. If they said that to me now, I don't think it'd make me upset.

---

49. I remember when I was nine† and realized I had consciousness. I remember vividly remembering just a couple years earlier when I had merely existed without being able to self-reflect. This terrified me. The ability to self-reflect I assumed was my soul. I assumed this meant that my soul had a beginning and therefore would have an end.

† See footnote 8.

Chapter Twenty-Five
Paris est une Fête

*C*aleb's favorite things in the world included thrift stores, flea markets, and yard sales. One of our favorite activities in Bloomington, as well as in Boston, had been to go to Goodwill and buy knickknacks, ephemera, and curios to use in our art projects, or, in Caleb's case, just to keep and possibly display around the house as objets trouvés.

Before Julian left, he told us about an incredible outdoor flea market he'd gone to when he first arrived in Paris. It took place from 10:00h—14:00h every Saturday and Sunday and spanned two full blocks in the far south of the city.

On Saturday, after settling in at Agnès's place and getting cleaned up, Caleb and I had enjoyed a grey afternoon being proper tourists. We'd visited the Pompidou and walked through the fourth arrondissement to Notre-Dame, then crossed the Seine and spent some time in Saint-Michel. We stopped for a late lunch. I ate a duck leg with skin caramelized in its own fat and Caleb ate a cheese omelet and bread and butter. Then we walked through the Latin Quarter of the Left Bank and stopped in the churches of Saint-Germaine and Saint-Sulpice, where Caleb took pictures.

We talked a few times about finding lipstick and going back to Père Lachaise, but it was raining intermittently and I didn't want either of us to spend the majority of our time in France trudging through a damp graveyard wrapped up in one of my compulsive Ahab-esque meta-crusades. I wanted us to sip espresso in cafés and take strolls along the Seine like normal Americans in Paris.

Plus, every time I thought of the bathetic failure of our first attempt to make a statement, my stomach hurt and I felt like throwing up.

Saturday night we'd finally gotten some sleep. Dareka was going out dancing and Agnès was going out to some party with an ambiguously romantic male friend, but Caleb and I stayed around her neighborhood in Oberkampf, ate street crêpes for dinner, and went to bed early.

On Sunday morning, well-rested at last, we trekked out to the flea market. I was looking for two things: one, a vintage men's velvet blazer, which Dareka had said would be easy to find at a French thrift store; and two, an antique brass statue of Shiva.

The first booth we passed displayed three full tables of Hindu and Buddhist deities. There was one tarnished Shiva about 18cm tall. It was Shiva as Nataraja, Lord of the Dancers, spinning inside a ring of fire. The owner, a relaxed gentleman of about fifty, said it was from the 1920s. It was just what I was looking for, but I told him I wanted walk around to a few other booths before I bought the first thing I saw.

In the beginning we spent several minutes at each booth pouring over the varied objects, but when a half hour had passed and we'd only moved about ten meters, we started to make quicker judgments. Caleb found two crucifixes he liked and a tiny, antique painting of a child on a piece of wood. Then we found a vintage clothing dealer with racks upon racks of velvet blazers.

I tried on about a dozen until I found one that fit, shoulders, hips, chest and all. It was sleek and oil-black. When I put it on and looked into the flimsy full-length mirror they had hanging from the end of the coat rack, I didn't look like Bob Dylan anymore. I looked like Arthur Rimbaud.

It's kind of expensive, I said, which was true. It was fifty euros, and Dareka had told me I shouldn't pay more than thirty.

I don't care, said Caleb. *You need to get that. You're not going to find a better one, and you look ridiculously hot.*

I bought the blazer[50] and thought of Patti Smith talking about dressing like Oscar Wilde and Arthur Rimbaud in the sixties. She said that the sixties were the first time people had dressed like people from other times. I didn't know if that was true, but in 2012, I didn't think it was possible not to dress like people from other times.

By the time we made it to the end of the market, some of the vendors were already packing up. It was almost 14:00h. I hadn't seen another statue of Shiva the whole two blocks.

We walked as quickly as we could back through all the tables to catch the gentleman with the Hindu statues. He was mostly packed up, but he remembered me on sight.

Shiva? he said, and opened up a large Rubbermaid box. Shiva was lying on top of a bed of newsprint.

Oui, merci, I said. *Soixante-dix euro, oui?*

He shrugged. *Cinquante.*

Vraiment?

Oui. Vraiment.

---

50. The purchase of the blazer, and the exchange with Caleb, actually happened earlier at a thrift store in Reims, but it fit better into the narrative here. The account of the purchase of Shiva takes no license.

I gave him the fifty euros and he wrapped Shiva up in newsprint. I looked at the dull brown of the antique brass as he folded it into the paper.

On peut le nettoyer? I said.

The man paused as if he were confused. *Oui. On peut le polir si tu veux.*

Do you think it would be hard to polish? I asked Caleb.

Caleb shrugged. *I think things look cool when they look old.*

The man handed me the wrapped piece, and I put it in my bag. I could feel its weight all the way back to Oberkampf.

That evening, while Dareka, Agnés, and the other six members of their eclectic band were practicing, I took Caleb out to dinner[51]. Since we'd lived in Boston, he'd consistently been the one to take me out since his income had generally been more reliable than mine. Now, with my grant money, plus hundreds of euros in cash in my pocket, I could finally sit down across from him and say, *Order anything you want. I've got it.*

We split a half-carafe of wine (which meant I drank a half-carafe of wine), a basket of pommes frites, and a basket of bread and butter. There was a vegetarian pasta dish on the menu that Caleb could eat, and I tried andouillette, which the waiter described to me in French as "very French," and which, as far as I could make out when it arrived, was a sausage casing stuffed entirely with some type of mammalian intestines.

As I slathered a forkful of sausage with mustard, I looked at Caleb and said, *So since we're in France and I'm taking you out to dinner, can I ask you a question, and then we can never speak of it again?*

---

51. I'm ninety percent positive that the restaurant, just down the hill from the band's practice space, was one I'd gone to with Thade in 2006. Multiple landmarks, a memorably awkward building shape, and uniquely tasty pommes frites corroborate this belief.

He choked a little as his fork clinked down onto his plate, then swallowed and looked away with an apprehensive half-laugh. A few moments passed, and then he said, tentatively, *Sure,* with an inflection that made it sound like a question.

I realized that he was worried I was going to tell him I was in love with him. That was not what I was going to say, but I could see why[52] he would be worried it was.

What I was going to say, and what I said, was, *Do you think I did the right thing breaking up with Thade?*

He let out a relieved breath and laughed a little. *Oh, that? Yeah, of course. Is that even still a question for you?*

No, I said. *Not usually. But you know, I'm gonna be thirty next year, and I wonder if that was like, my one chance for that type of relationship. Actually, I know that was my one chance for that type of relationship. Even if I met someone now and we spent the rest of our lives together, it's different to meet someone when you're already a grownup, when you've already solidified as a person somewhat, versus when you're still forming. They'll never know me when I was still forming. My stories will always just be stories to them. They won't have lived it with me.*

Caleb shook his head. *Well, even if that's true, it seems like you're a way happier person without him. You're way nicer, at least, if that's any indication.*

No, I know. You're right. I tore a piece off my paper napkin and blew my nose.

And besides, he said, picking up his fork and carefully stabbing pasta, *you're always the one to break things off with people from what I've seen. No one ever breaks up with you. They may not be what you want, but you're the one who always walks away.*

---

52. *It is quite true that I have worshiped you with far more romance of feeling than a man usually gives to a friend. From the moment we met, your personality had the most extraordinary influence over me. I quite admit that I adored you madly, extravagantly, absurdly. I was jealous of everyone to whom you spoke. I wanted to have you all to myself. I was only happy when I was with you. When I was away from you, you were still present in my art.* —O.W., The Picture of Dorian Gray

I smeared two thick frites in the meat juices on my plate with my fork. *Huh,* I said. *I guess you're right.* I chewed the crispy, salty potatoes and swallowed. *Maybe I don't actually want what I think I want.*

Caleb shrugged. *Maybe not.*

We didn't talk much for the rest of dinner. One of the things I'd always appreciated about our friendship was our economy with words. We spoke when we needed to tell the other something. Other than that it was enough just to know the other was there.

When he first told me he was going to come with me on tour, I didn't believe him. People are always saying they're going to do stuff like that on a Wednesday afternoon when you're eating sea salt brownies on the sofa watching a Woody Allen movie about Paris, but no one ever really follows through.

Caleb did. He used the last of the Dead Mom Money (DMM) that he'd received on his thirtieth birthday. When I was twenty-three and he was twenty-four, he told me about this relatively modest inheritance. It was set up so he'd receive one-third when he turned twenty-five, one-third when he turned twenty-seven-and-a-half, and the final one-third when he turned thirty.

At alcoholic, depressive twenty-three, the notion that either one of us would live long enough to enjoy the last of Caleb's DMM seemed completely absurd to me. If you'd told me what he would use the last of his DMM for when we were mod-podging porno-collages in his living room in Bloomington, I wouldn't even have known how to understand you.

I piled mustard on a large chunk of andouillette. Caleb put down his fork on his half-finished pasta and pushed the plate away from him. I've always had about twice Caleb's appetite. He leaned his forearms on the table and clasped his hands tensely waiting for me to finish. I swallowed the rest of my wine and noticed the tattoos on his arms. His mother's reminders. *Remember death. Seize the day.*

Chapter Twenty-Six
Montmartre

*L*ate Monday morning, I bought red lipstick from a department store across from the Moulin Rouge while Caleb browsed the sex toy shop a block down. I knew, from my trip in 2006, that it was possible to walk from Pigalle to Montmartre and then to Basilique du Sacré-Cœur, whose dome I'd seen alighted at night but had never been inside.

What I didn't remember was that Montmartre and Sacré-Cœur were at the highest points of Paris and that the walk was a progressively steep uphill climb. The days of walking, churches, museums[53], and uneven streets had taken their toll on my left leg. Earlier that morning, watched with interest by Agnès's incontinent cat, I'd done some yoga poses to try to ease the cramping, but I still walked with a noticeable limp.

As we walked up the hill I thought of Gertrude Stein walking daily up to Montmartre from her apartment at 27 rue des Fleurus to sit for Picasso as he painted her portrait. The walk must have taken her

---

53. The day before, in the Pompidou, I'd put the heel of my left cowboy boot up on a chair to try to readjust my bones' alignment and the guard reprimanded me in four languages, much to Caleb's mortification.

an hour each way. She would compose sentences in her head as she walked. Picasso was young and poor at the time, struggling alongside Matisse and so many other now-revered artists to find ways to support themselves through their art.

When we reached the main square, artists had set up their easels among the many gift shops overflowing with cheap incidentals, trinkets, and knickknacks. The artists advertised caricatures. Thirty euro and twenty-five minutes and tourists could go to dinner with their own cartoon portrait under their arm. Three artists were actively working on tourists' caricatures as we walked by. We stopped to take in the kitsch.

It's so funny, I said. *In Picasso's time, Montmartre was like Brooklyn ten years ago. A cheap neighborhood that artists could afford that became a cradle of authentic creative activity.*

Caleb looked at me skeptically. *What do you mean, "authentic?"*

I watched an artist as his fingers began to create form out of lines. *I'm not sure, exactly. I just know that after the authenticity blossomed, the money found it and the creativity died. Look. Montmartre became a relic of itself. Caricatures instead of portraits. Shallow, cartoonish imitations of whatever the authenticity here was. Authenticity is attractive but dangerous. You need to embrace uncertainty and unknowing and, if you believe all the world's saints, yogis, and mystics, some form of poverty. Ownership, status, security, all of it—they all require and cultivate quite a bit of affected protective scaffolding. When these pretenses are stripped away, an artist can speak with honesty, not as a name, a job, or a gender, but as a human being.*

Gentrification happens when people in society recognize and are attracted to this honesty. They want to stay in their structures of name, job, and gender, but they still crave tastes of this essential humanness. They understand it on some level because, by its very nature, it's universal. But they haven't done the work to experience it themselves. Then they don't really understand what it is they're attracted to, so they tend to mistake the superficial characteristics of the movement in question—Cubism, Modernism, Beat Poetry, Mersey Beat, etc.—with the honesty itself. When the authentic art flees to its new blank, impoverished space, the money seizes the location and look of the particular movement, simplifies and sanitizes it, and packages it for safe consumption by earnest tourists.

Caleb shrugged. *I don't know. I think you can make money and still make good art. The hope is that you find something that feels authentic and true but then also sells. Selling is a way to show relevance.*

The artist I was watching handed a flattering caricature to a grinning teenage girl. *Hmm,* I said.

There were tourists everywhere: spilling out of the cafés and gift shops; bumping into us with plastic bags full of souvenir J'♥ Paris t-shirts and berets; and taking pictures with professional cameras and point-and-shoots and countless smart phones. Whenever someone bumped into me, I had to stop and crack my left knee to realign it.

Caleb clutched his camera bag to his chest, both shoulders pulled up near his ears.

Let's get out of here and see the church, I said.

Yeah, he said.

I didn't know where we were going, but I had a faint understanding that we should continue to walk uphill. A few blocks out from the tourist maelstrom, the streets grew quiet again, the shops and boulangeries appearing to cater to local residents rather than foreigners.

In front of a steep staircase that ran through a nearly vertical park, I asked a forty-something Parisian-looking woman which way was Sacré-Cœur.

Ah non, she said. *Je ne suis pas une carte. Pas de tout.*

Quoi? I said.

She said she's not a map, Caleb said.

Oh, I said. *D'accord. Merci.*

We continued to walk uphill until we saw the Basilique's dome rising above the rooftops. We climbed up the staircase and paused in front of the entrance to look out over the city's streets spreading in front of us in organic fractal patterns. I could see Notre-Dame and the Seine, Saint-Michel and the Left Bank. The sun was dodging in and out of holes in the clouds. It was the first time I'd seen a blue sky since being in Paris.

According to stories, it took Gertrude Stein a while to figure out romance. In her late twenties, she dropped out of medical school because of personal tumult stemming from an unrealized attraction to one of her female classmates. Then, finally, in her early thirties, she met Alice B. Toklas, and they of course stayed together[54] until Gertrude Stein died.

They weren't yet famous when Gertrude Stein wrote *The Autobiography of Alice B. Toklas.* It was the book that made them famous. The book itself made them famous because Gertrude Stein used the book to tell the world they should be so.

Gertrude Stein told the world they should be famous by using her most intimate relationship as a mirror to see herself. The story is not Gertrude Stein or Alice B. Toklas, but Gertrude Stein as she was to Alice B. Toklas as she was to Gertrude Stein. It was only through her eyes that she could honestly see. No one knew Gertrude like Alice and no one knew Alice like Gertrude and what you read is that knowing.

Before we walked into Sacré-Cœur, Caleb said, *You know, we could still go back to the grave, as long as we don't spend forever in here.*

Yeah, I said, as we ascended the towering staircase. *Maybe. Let's see how we feel if there's time.*

---

54. The fact that Gertrude Stein associated genius with masculinity, and that Alice was largely relegated to the role of hostess at the couple's famous salons, entertaining the wives in the next room while the "men" debated, is sometimes difficult for me to reconcile and at other times makes perfect sense.

Cahpter Twenty-Seven
Sacré-Cœur

The stage is bare except for a sign upstage right that reads AUCUNE PHOTOGRAPHIE. JADE enters upstage left and walks to center, pausing to cross herself before continuing to walk downstage. A CROWD of tourists, including CALEB, continuously process behind JADE, left to right, as stage lights dim, about half of them pausing when they pass center to cross themselves. JADE walks with a slight limp into a spotlight, center stage, and addresses the AUDIENCE, which occupies the position of the bema, altar, and mural of the Holy Trinity.

JADE

[Takes a tissue from pocket. Blows nose.]

AUDIENCE

Why are you here?

JADE

Aren't I supposed to ask you that?

AUDIENCE

It would be the same question, and you would get the same answer. Why are you here?

JADE

What do you mean, *here?* Why am I on the planet, why am I in Paris, or why am I in this church?

AUDIENCE

It's all the same question.

JADE

[Pause.] When I was a child, I thought I was destined to be some sort of historical something. I believed I would find something profound to say and would say it and that it would change, somehow, the face of the world. When I got older, I realized that this feeling didn't make me special. That lots of people feel this way when they're young, and then they, as they say, "grow out of it."

AUDIENCE

You did not grow out of it.

JADE

I don't know if that means there's something wrong with me or not. I still think every breath I take is somehow important, even though at the same time I know it makes me just like everyone else.

AUDIENCE

Can't it be both?

JADE

I think everything's always both.

AUDIENCE

Existence is composed by the interplay of opposites.

JADE

When I was at my lowest point in the Psych Ward there were a couple of hours in which I truly believed I was the Divine Incarnation, Jesus Christ, or whatever. I looked at the flesh of my hands covering the muscle and bone and knew deep down that I was (G/g)od.

AUDIENCE

You romanticize your time in the Psych Ward when you tell the story, you know. You were only there for three days. Your parents drove down from Indianapolis and visited you every afternoon. And when you took all those pills, you called your friends right away. You never really wanted to die.

JADE

To be alive is to be divine. Am I a kind of Jesus in the sense that I've used my flesh to act out myth? I've taken all I have, my only life, and thrown all of it into this idea. Anyone who really lives is really Christ.

AUDIENCE

What is really living?

JADE

What anyone great—and I don't just mean like Oscar Wilde or Gertrude Stein or Arthur Rimbaud or Patti Smith or whatever, I mean also just like great teachers or great mothers or great bartenders or anyone—has done. Committed themselves fully to their flesh as it played out its character moving through time and space and relationships.

AUDIENCE

Did/do you choose your character?

JADE

When I was twenty-two, three years after I'd been in the Psych Ward, I wanted to kill myself again. I was finally normal. I had a recognizable role—someone's girlfriend in a town in Indiana. I was living a small, safe life, but I could find no meaning in it. I couldn't see any future for the person I was, and so I thought I wanted to die. After lying in bed for two weeks in the middle of a sweltering summer, it was clear I had a choice between jumping into the river or jumping into the unknown. Instead of killing myself, I decided to change myself completely. I did an out-of-character thing—something I would never do— and in doing so, I created a new character for myself. The desire to kill myself was just my noticing that I was already dead. I didn't have to die, I just had to accept the end of a certain story and begin the next one. The story of me I'd been living had developed and completed its plot arch. It was resolved. It was already a corpse. [Blows nose.]

AUDIENCE

You're talking about when you and Thade were sitting slumped against opposite walls in the dining room. You were both crying too hard to speak. Do you remember?

JADE

Yes.

AUDIENCE

You saw something.

JADE

Yes.

AUDIENCE

What did you see?

JADE

I saw two stories of my life, running parallel, like two simultaneously playing films. In one, I stayed and had a shared bed and a sublanguage of inside jokes and comfortable walls, and in the other, I left and was what I am now. They were both real, and they both depended on whether I said yes or whether I said no.

AUDIENCE

What makes you think you're so special?

JADE

I don't know. Being talented means nothing. There are a million talented people. Being smart means nothing. There are a million smart people. I think if it's anything it's that my body kept rejecting the other life. I was sick all the time. I could barely breathe. I tried to kill myself once, and thought about it many, many more times. Maybe you can only become an artist by default. The only people who actually become artists are people for whom it's the only alternative to death. We must create or we must die. We must die or we must create.

AUDIENCE

And why not death?

JADE

Why not life? If it doesn't matter, if I'm going to die anyway, I may as well throw myself into this absurd romance. [Blows nose.] Besides, if I don't, who's going to?

AUDIENCE

Have you been alone?

JADE

Yes. It feels like always.

AUDIENCE

What is it like?

JADE

Like Oscar Wilde in Reading Gaol.

AUDIENCE

No, not for Oscar Wilde or Gertrude Stein or Allen Ginsberg or Bob Dylan or Patti Smith or Arthur fucking Rimbaud. What is it like for *you*?

JADE

I don't know if I know the difference. I dreamed of being a poet in Paris a hundred times before actually getting here, through the stories of people who did it before me or who dreamed of doing it before me. I learned about love from watching Woody Allen movies and 70s sitcoms on Nick at Nite. I don't know if I know how to experience something for the first time.

AUDIENCE
Let's put it this way. In being alone, what have you found?

JADE
Sometimes God. Sometimes the Absence of god.

AUDIENCE
You have to unpack that for us.

JADE
[Blows nose.] At night lately, trying to sleep without having a drink, I feel the same inside of myself and outside of myself until it almost seems like my skin could melt or is melting, and it seems like it's that that we're always trying to get back to as we spread out and the universe spreads out and it's that that we're really thinking about when we call someone late at night or scribble some silly rhyming poem about breath or carry our blankets out from our bedrooms to the sofa and try to find comfort in the discomfort and are reminded of some feeling of safety we think we had as children even though as children we all knew very well the imperfectness of our homes and that the home we're always trying to get back to didn't exactly ever exist, but was maybe always just the place before we were born and also after we die and also all around and within always and how this is why we travel over oceans and descend into catacombs and take drugs and dance till we drip sweat and get married and have children and write books and build cities, their stone always eroding but stronger than us, we can imagine a little at least.

AUDIENCE

Is that all?

JADE

Yes. Maybe that. Or maybe just that that thing I'd called (G/g)od was always only me all along.

Chapter Twenty-Eight
De Profundis

It was late afternoon when we got back to Agnès's apartment post-Sacré-Cœur, and we didn't need to be at the Downtown Cafe until 19:00h. Agnès lived in Oberkampf, the same neighborhood where the Downtown Café was, which was where my last show was that night (Monday), which was our last night in Paris. The closest Metro station to Agnès was Menilmontant, which was one stop away from Père Lachaise. We still had time to make it back to the cemetery before sundown.

Caleb grabbed an extra battery pack and his gloves, and I switched the gold suede coat I'd worn in Montmartre for my new velvet blazer. In the blazer's left pocket, I placed the lipstick I'd bought in Pigalle and a folded paper copy of my poem, "Kissing Oscar Wilde." In the blazer's right pocket, I placed the heart-shaped rock from Gertrude Stein's grave and ran it over and over in my hand as we walked wordlessly to the Metro station. We rode one stop wordlessly. We wordlessly walked up the steps and through the gates and read the posted map. We spoke to orient ourselves and plan our route, and then we walked in silence.

The graveyard was emptier than it had been on Friday. We crossed paths with a few small clusters of tourists who asked us in French and then in English if we knew how to find Jim Morrison's grave. We did not. There also may have been an odd local or two out walking a tiny dog or two through the city of tombs. I barely noticed. All I could see or think of seeing was Oscar.

We arrived. The grave was not different. It was spotless and grey surrounded by four glass walls. The glass was smeared with makeup, saliva, and the oil of human skin. The sun was breaking through the clouds, and its golden beams slanted across our bodies and cut through the smeared glass, speckling the stone angel with cold shadow and warm light.

No one else was around. We couldn't even hear anyone walking through the grass or talking. The light glimmered and danced across our skin and my velvet blazer and the earth. We stood there for a few moments just watching the light move and the grave not move against the movement of the light.

I took out my lipstick and Caleb took out his camera. I slid the sweet-scented waxy red across my mouth in two circles. I stood for a moment more while Caleb readied his stance over my left shoulder. Then I stepped forward and kissed the glass.

I held the kiss, listening to the soft sound of Caleb's shutter fire once, twice, three times. I held the kiss. The shutter fired a fourth and fifth time.

Hold on, he said. *Let me try from over here.*

I let the kiss go and looked at its red flower print as Caleb walked around to the side of the tomb. *Okay, try now,* he said, positioning his camera so that it aimed at my face through the two walls of glass. I reapplied the lipstick and kissed again a few inches from the first kiss and listened to the sound of Caleb's shutter fire and fire and pause and fire.

I raised the hand that held the lipstick a few more inches so Caleb could fit it into the frame. He didn't have to tell me how to move. I knew how he saw me and could almost see the shot as I kissed. He would move slightly and I would move slightly, and he would shoot and we would both slightly move again.

This was about love, though it felt awkward. This felt awkward, though it was about love. This was false. I was kissing, yes, but I was posing. This was true. I was posing, yes, but I was kissing.

Who was I kissing for? I felt Caleb and felt Caleb see me, and for a moment, he and I become the same person and I felt the space between us hold both of us and Oscar Wilde and Patti Smith and Arthur Rimbaud and my mother and father and Thade reading on our front porch in Bloomington and Louis pontificating on the Harvard footbridge and Marissa breathing in her inviolable teenage bed and everyone I'd ever loved and Everyone and Nothingness and Beauty and the Absence of god. My skin melted away and became the same as the glass and the tomb and the air between the glass and the tomb. I was not. I was all.

Who was I posing for? Who was I to think anyone would want to look at me kissing the same spot a thousand—ten thousand other people had kissed? I wasn't a movie star or even a famous writer, and Oscar Wilde had been dead for a hundred years. What did I think we were going to do with these pictures? Who did I think I was?

Caleb took a few more pictures, and I felt him stop. He stood with a certain bored tenseness when he'd exhausted a shot. I opened my eyes and stood back and looked at him through the pane. He took one more picture and then walked back to the front of the tomb and stood behind me.

The nearly setting sun brought slight movement to the cemetery. The tourists and dog-walkers were beginning their slow centrifugal meander. I took another look at the glass-encased monument. It didn't feel complete, our interaction, whatever it was. I uncapped the lipstick and wrote in cursive the only word I could think of: amour. I heard Caleb take a picture. When I was finished I looked at the word across the smeared glass and was embarrassed by my lack of originality.

The sun was gone again, and the air was cooling. Caleb looked unsatisfied. He had wanted, as I had wanted, for me to have some sort of profound moment of revelation or closure at the grave. He wanted this, I knew, because he loved me, and taking pictures was how he knew how to show it. We left Père Lachaise in silence, walking slowly side by side. It didn't feel complete, really, or even okay, but we'd done what we came to do. It was either earnest vanity or vain earnestness. It was both vainly earnest and earnestly vain.

Chapter Twenty-Nine
Les Deux Mondes

We walked in to oily smoke spilling out of the kitchen. Agnès was frying frozen crêpes in slippers and a robe.

Hi! I called.

She glanced toward us for a cursory instant. *Hello. How was your day?*

Um, great, I said, taking off my scarf and boots by the front door. *We went to Montmartre and Sacré-Cœur.*

Ah, yes. Good good. And you have your last show tonight, yes? Downtown Café?

Yes. I'm not quite sure where it is, but I can just text Dareka.

It's easy. A five minute walk from here. I can tell you.

Oh okay. Are you going to come?

She rested her plastic turner against the edge of the hot frying pan. *I don't know. Not after the way practice went last night.* She picked the turner back up and scooped the crêpes up onto a plate, turned off the heat, and ran the pan under the faucet. The whole apartment filled with steam. She sat down at the kitchen table with her plate and took a bite. *If I do go, I'll go later. I need to relax for a bit and smoke. You won't go on until at least 10 o'clock.*

While Agnès ate and smoked a joint, Caleb and I showered and changed. I wore a checked collared shirt with my *MUSTACHE RIDES*-pinned sweater vest and a skinny red and black plaid tie that Caleb tied for me on his neck and then placed around my neck. I topped it off with my velvet blazer.

Agnès was draped over her sofa, trumpet-heavy jazz wailing out of the speakers in her living room, as we stood ready with my little bag of books and Caleb's camera bag. She became briefly vertical enough to draw us a simple map showing us the way to the Downtown Café, then stretched back out again.

The walk took somewhat longer than five minutes, as I frequently had to stop and readjust my left knee. Caleb was used to this stop-and-go and simply walked when I walked and stopped when I stopped.

I realized half a block from the venue that we hadn't eaten since before Montmartre. *Are you hungry?* I said. *Do you need food?*

I'll be okay, said Caleb.

The Downtown Café was a mid-to-upscale bar with tall, dark wood chairs and tables. The stage was in front of the large windows that overlooked the street, busy even on a Monday with hip foot traffic.

Dareka was already there when we arrived, standing the center of a small cluster of beautiful, pale Parisian poets, gesturing with a half-full bottle of Coca-Cola. When he saw us, he waved me over. I walked over and we bisou'd and he put his hand on my shoulder and introduced me to all of the French poets and we all bisou'd and I learned all of their names and forgot all of their names.

Then Dareka led me over to the stage, where a tall, slender man in a golf-cap was standing.

This is Clément, AKA the Good Slamaritan. He is my partner in running this venue.

Nice to meet you, said Clément.

Nice to meet you.

We shook hands and bisou'd. Clément didn't look much like the other venue organizers, who were all aged somewhere between mid-twenties and mid-thirties. Clément was well over forty, with thinning, dark grey hair and a clean-shaven face, slim and large-nosed with big deep pools of eyes. His English was flawless, and his expressive face was calm and kind.

Caleb was suddenly standing behind me. *Jade,* he said.

I turned. *Yeah?*

He gestured to the wall behind him. *Look who's here.* I looked. Adélaïde was sitting behind a long table along the wall, Humphrey Bogart hat and all.

For a moment, I didn't move. She smiled big and waved when she saw us. This was real. She was here. We went over to where she was sitting and I bisou'd her and even Caleb bisou'd her.

Thank you so much for coming! I said. *I'd forgotten you'd even be in Paris for this. I would have invited you if I'd remembered.*

I came up last night, she said. *I was excitated when I saw you would be here. My friend apartment I'm staying is not so far.*

She was holding a box of cookies in her lap and a pen in her hand, a paper notebook opened on the table in front of her along with a wadded up tissue. Next to the notebook was a full shopping bag with a small bunch of bananas on top. She offered us each a cookie, and we ate them. Then she offered us each a banana, and we ate them, too.

My mother sent this with me, she said. *She is afraid I will starve to death in the city, apparently.*

Thank you, I said. *We didn't get to eat dinner. We've been running around all day.*

You did not eat? Oh here, have more biscuits. She opened the box of cookies and set them out on the table. *I'm excitated to see you perform again*, she said. Caleb and I both took more cookies and started to eat.

And you, she said, leaning into Caleb. *I looked on your website of your photograph.* She placed her hand on his forearm. *I hope you understand, I am in love.*

Caleb blushed and shrugged, covering his chewing mouth with his hand. I felt pricks of jealousy rise from between my shoulder blades and up my spine. I did not like or want the jealousy, and I couldn't tell to which direction, if any, it was directed or attached. I told it to quiet down, and it quieted down. I sat down on the other side of Adélaïde so that she was in between me and Caleb.

What did you do today so you were too busy to eat? she asked.

I swallowed my third cookie. *Caleb and I went to Père Lachaise to visit Oscar Wilde.*

Her eyes widened. *Oscar Wilde? He's one of my favorites in English. In Dublin there is a statue of him. I have in my computer a picture of me kissing his nose.*

Aw, I said. *That's so sweet.*

Yes, only I was there with my gay friend. He kissed him too… only in another place.

Caleb laughed. *Awesome.*

Yes. She shrugged. *I wanted to show that picture to my mother, though.*

Are you going to perform? I asked.

I don't know, she said. *I think maybe I will just watch tonight. To see how the writing is here. Maybe then I will perform next week. Do you know what you will do?*

I guess just the same poems I've been doing, I said.

Will you do the one which rhymed?

"On Breathing?" Yes, I'll do *"On Breathing."*

Ah, good.

There was a pause, and I felt like I needed to blow my nose. I reached into my right pocket for a tissue, and instead found Gertrude Stein's rock heart. Then I remembered the lipstick and poem in my left pocket.

Actually, I have this one, too, I said, pulling out the folded sheet of paper. *It's not in the books I brought. It's brand new. I wrote it right before I left. It's about Oscar Wilde and how they cleaned his grave of all the kiss marks.*

I handed her the poem and she began to read. I wasn't sure if it was too dense for someone whose native language wasn't English, but she seemed to make her way though it without too much trouble.

She pointed to the line, "I worry I've outlived the romantics," and said, *Thank you for writing this. I have felt this so many times.*

The night began. The audience was a tightly-packed crowd of about fifty. A medley of local writers performed a piece apiece. Several, including Clément, performed hip-hop, others recited inciting, dramatic monologues, and others read quiet, delicate poems off trembling sheets of paper. Dareka performed a rhyming piece accompanied by a short, mohawked girl on an accordion. Shortly before my set, Agnès showed up, transforming the whole crowd into an impromptu beatbox as she freestyle rapped.

Caleb stood behind the mostly-seated crowd to shoot my set. I performed "Plates," followed by Dareka's reading of "Assiettes" in French. It was not quite The Magic, but the audience was perfectly quiet and I could feel they were with me. I read "Kissing Oscar Wilde" in English, but most of it was lost on the crowd. I ended with "On Breathing," performed in English clearly and rhythmically. At the end of my set, the room was silent for several seconds. Then, the audience stood up to applaud.

Merci, I said. *Merci beaucoup. Je vous aime. Vraiment. Vous êtes fantastiques. Merci bien.*

I sat back down next to Adélaïde, body vibrating. Caleb sat on the other side of me so that I was sandwiched in between them. We sat like this for the last third of the show. Adélaïde took Caleb's camera (which I'd never seen anyone try to do before) and took pictures of me and Caleb. She took several before she set the camera down and gave me a thin Italian paper notebook[55]. It was blank inside, and its cover was printed with bright red flowers. I gave her[56] the paper copy of "Kissing Oscar Wilde." I blew my nose, and she blew her nose. Caleb took his camera back and took pictures of me and Adélaïde. In one, she doesn't know her picture's being taken, and she's smiling. In another, she knows her picture's being taken, and she's grimacing like a kabuki mask.

Half of me imagined what would happen if I kissed Adélaïde or if Adélaïde kissed me. What if we stumbled back clutching hands to the room where she was staying and fell onto her bed in a tangle of breathless limbs? What if I missed my flight the next morning? What if we wrote to one another across continents for months, peeling back layer after layer of personality until we each revealed that hollow space where she and I were the same and therefore not alone? What if, at last, we decided that we couldn't bear to be apart for another instant, and we flew to one another and got married[57] right away in Massachusetts and in France so we could split our time between the countries and I

---

55. This notebook is where I started to draft many of the words that became this book.

56. Of course, the "you" in the poem was Louis, originally, though I had barely thought about him in weeks. Now here I was, giving it to Adélaïde, intending it to be for Adélaïde. It was weird for a moment, then I decided to let it not be weird.

57. Or what if circumstances (money, work, etc.) kept us tragically apart? What if all we had was that/this one night in Paris?

could write and she could act and we could bake bread and keep small dogs and hold fantastic artist salons like Gertrude Stein and Alice.

Adélaïde scrolled through the images on Caleb's camera and laughed her fox bark laugh. Over her shoulder, I saw one she'd taken. A rare picture of Caleb and me in frame together[58]. For an instant, I tried to imagine what our friendship would look like if it weren't for Patti Smith. Would he be here now taking pictures? Would he have started taking pictures of me at all?

I looked back at Adélaïde in her *Casablanca* hat. I hardly knew anything about this person. I didn't want to try to pull her into a film or graft her onto the skeleton of some idealized icon. I didn't even know if she was queer at all. When she lifted her gaze from the camera, she smiled at me with that one, asymmetrical dimple. If there was a moment to ask if I could kiss her, which I'm not sure if there was, this would have been it. Instead, I smiled back silently. That was all.

After the show, someone bought me a cordial glass full of a local, anise-flavored liqueur, which I sipped. It made me immediately sleepy.

I said goodbye to Adélaïde with three bisous and one hug. I may have lingered ever so slightly as my lips met the soft of her cheek or as we pressed our bodies into one another. I may have wanted, for one final flash, that fantastic, literary romance. For that I blame the liqueur, or the poetry, or Paris. Before she left she wrote down her address. Caleb told her he would mail her a plastic camera, and I told her I would send her a copy of *Just Kids*. She disappeared in time to catch the last train. I watched her walk away, a slender, hunched silhouette lit by streetlights and neon. I let this moment be perfect.

Outside, a small crowd had gathered to meet me and talk about the performance. I sold the last of my books. We left in a shower of bisous.

---

58. In the picture, I'm conspicuously leering at Adélaïde. Caleb is out of focus behind me, though bright-eyed and actually smiling.

Agnès led us back to her apartment. She offered several compliments about my set as we walked, but I didn't have the energy to answer with anything more than, *Thank you. Thank you so much.*

I started undressing as soon as the door to our guest room was closed, peeling off the vest and freeing my neck from the tie before dropping my pants, shirt, and bra to the floor. Caleb put on his pajamas in the corner of the room, his back turned toward me as he changed shirts. I slipped into my soft purple Barcelona Poetry Slam t-shirt and boxers, and Caleb and I set to making sure everything was packed and ready for the flight in the morning.

It wasn't just my left leg. My whole body was sore and exhausted. No bed had ever felt so good.

Oh my god, I said as I slid under the sheets. *I'm so fucking tired.* I curled my body into a careful fetal position, my back to Caleb. *Why did I want to be an artist?* I said. *It's so exhausting.*

Everything else is exhausting, too, he said. *It's just not rewarding.*

If I said anything after that, I don't remember. When Caleb was settled in, I turned out the light and we lay there, our backs to one another, the warmth of our bodies and the quiet movement of our breaths all that let each other know the other was there.

Chapter Thirty
Charles de Gaulle

t was just a few minutes past 07:00h, and from the way sun was negotiating the silver gossamer of the clouds, it looked as though it might turn into a blue-sky day. I ate a fat, café-frosted phallus of an éclair, and Caleb ate a flaky croissant au beurre from a Menilmontant patisserie before we got on the Metro that would take us to the train that would take us to the airport. I stood and looked at the just-waking streets before we went underground. All around us, black-coated Parisians walked to work or the café or the Metro, several with tiny dogs, many smoking cigarettes, many eating breakfast pastries wrapped in butter-splotched paper. I knew I could live a whole life here. I could let my body melt into the tall boots and the sleek silhouettes of dark French fashion. Learn to play the accordion. Take up smoking. This fantasia played for few moments before Caleb and the chill of the air against my skin reminded me of where I was in time and space. *We should go,* said Caleb. *I don't know how long we'll have to wait for the second train.*

We rode through the graffittied parts of Paris above ground. Whenever I leave a city, I watch it for as long as I can, like it's a person I love and may never see again. As we rode farther and farther away from the city's center, the buildings became short, spaced-out, unremarkable. I watched them until there was no trace of anything I recognized, until they could have been any suburb of Boston or Indianapolis or New York. Then I looked at Caleb. He was slumped into his seat, his arms folded across his torso, his eyes closed.

I said, *It's incredible how there are these currents running through human civilization all the time. That we can come to another country where they speak another language and meet these people, and connect through these, like, pre-established roles and understood relationships. The universe is vast and intricate and busy. It's amazing. It's beautiful.*

Caleb furrowed his brow and opened his eyes. *Um, I'm not sure if I know what you mean. I mean, of course people would bond over what they had in common. You're meeting a bunch of people through poetry, so they connect over poetry. In photography circles, people bond over photography. I'm sure in, like, football circles, people bond over football.*

No, I know. But, I mean... I trailed off and looked back out the window. *I guess I'm just not explaining it well, then.*

A minute passed. Maybe a minute and a half. I took a deep breath and tried again. *I mean, there seem to be these systems in place to hold these art forms—all of them, I'm not saying poetry's special, or art's special, or I'm special. I just mean it seems that there are these roles there to fill, and that people just kind of step into them in order to be them. Not just to play them, but to, like, be them. And it's almost incidental who does it. It almost seems arbitrary. Like anyone could do it if they just, like, did.*

Like, the world knows how to interact with a poet. Everyone knows that character should be there, so when someone steps in and says 'Hey, I'm a poet,' the world knows what to do. It's just no one ever thinks that they can be a poet. Almost since forever, people have thought poets were something that existed in some bygone era. Anyone who grew up saying they wanted to be a poet was told they were 'chasing the past,' or whatever. But we're not chasing anything. We're reliving the past, playing the same roles, and re-imagining them for our cultural contexts—our particular spots in time and space. And that's anyone's job as an artist. To retell the same stories people have always told for their particular context.

Caleb shrugged. *I don't know,* he said. *I don't know if I really see it that way.* I thought for a moment he was going to say something else, but he didn't. He just closed his eyes again, and I looked back out the window.

The soles of my cowboy boots slid along the slick tile of Charles de Gaulle as I dragged my suitcase behind me. My left leg was cramped, and I was looking forward to the eight-plus hours of sitting ahead of me.

We each got our boarding passes and went through security together. Caleb was flying direct on Air France and I was taking Air Canada through Montreal. We walked down terminal 2 and stopped at the division between 2A and 2E, facing one another.

Caleb shrugged and made that face. *See you back at home,* he said.

Yeah, I said. *Have a good flight.*

We crossed each other and walked down separate hallways. I was aware that this was the end of something. A story Caleb and I had begun together years earlier was drawing to its natural close. Not all love needs to be physical to be creative. Somehow I knew we had made something whole and complete together, and, from this moment forward, however our friendship would look, it would be different. Suddenly, I didn't feel as though I needed him to help carry so many parts of me. I was ready to try to hold myself on my own.

I bought a café americaine from a chain café next to my gate before boarding. The plane was only about half-sold, and I had a whole row of three seats to myself. I sat by the window.

As the plane took off, I looked at the people on the ground, each one moving through space, navigating and narrating a private universe of stor(y/ies). They grew tinier and tinier as we climbed until they were absorbed by the capillary web of streets that composed the city.

I watched the buildings, then the neighborhoods, and then the city itself as it shrank and curved with perspective. I saw Paris, then France, then Europe, then (E/e)arth. Eventually the land dropped into a dark blue ocean that bent heavily along the bright sky. I saw the whole world. It was very beautiful and very far away.

Jade et Adélaïde by Caleb Cole

Jade performs in Dijon by Caleb Cole

Dijon Street by Caleb Cole

Kissing the Glass by Caleb Cole

Writing by Caleb Cole

Jade and Caleb by Adélaïde Pornet

Acknowledgements

Several pieces of this book have been previously published in earlier forms. "We'll Always Have Paris," "Halloween," "An Epically Abridged Catalogue of the Author's Major Romances...," and the poem, "On Breathing," were all featured in *DigBoston*. "Jade is a Jade is a Jade is a Jade" appeared in *BuzzFeed LGBT* under the title, "I Hate Labels So Much I Decided to Change My Name." The poem, "Kissing Oscar Wilde" won the 2011 Bayou Poetry Prize, and was published in *Bayou Magazine*. The poetry tour this book is based on was partially funded by a travel grant from the Foundation for Contemporary Arts, and I wrote the first half of the first draft of this book in an apartment loaned to me by *Amethyst Arsenic*'s Somerhouse program. To everyone in each of these organizations who has believed in this project, I cannot thank you enough.

I would also like to pile heaps and heaps of love and thank yous on the following people:

Sam Cha for being a brain brother and the best writer I know. Dawn Gabriel for being the big sister I never knew I wanted. Ada and Alice for being tiny giant inspiration turbines. Samantha Milowsky for being one of the first people to make me feel legitimate. Simone Beaubien for having the space in Boston ready for my poetic fantasies to land. Sophia Cacciola and Michael J. Epstein for all the fun, artistic distractions while I was egomaniacally laboring over the earliest drafts of this thing. Eowyn for mitigating my panic while I was egomaniacally laboring over the latest drafts of this thing. Meff for getting it. My brother John for talking to me about physics on Google Chat when we're both up at 3AM. My parents for agreeing with me on almost nothing and loving me anyway. Leyna and Caleb for setting this wild story in motion and continuing to author it with me. Everyone above for all the meals and drinks and late-night conversations. Everyone I've ever loved for this.

About the Author

Jade Sylvan is the author of the poetry collection, *The Spark Singer,* and the fiction novels *TEN* and *Backstage at the Caribou.* Many of Jade's stories, essays, and poems have been published in places such as *PANK, Word Riot, BuzzFeed, DigBoston,* and others. Jade is also a performing artist, and regularly causes queer feminist performative trouble in the Northeast region of the United States, especially in the neighborhoods of Cambridge and Somerville, Massachusetts. Jade lives and works in Cambridge among a rotating cast of geniuses, fairies, magicians, and kings.

IF YOU LIKE JADE SYLVAN, JADE SYLVAN LIKES...

Uncontrolled Experiments in Freedom
Brian Ellis

The Incredible Sestina Anthology
Daniel Nester, Editor

Everything Is Everything
Cristin O'Keefe Aptowicz

The New Clean
Jon Sands

Bring Down the Chandeliers
Tara Hardy

Write Bloody Publishing distributes and promotes great books of fiction, poetry and art every year. We are an independent press dedicated to quality literature and book design, with an office in Austin, TX.

Our employees are authors and artists so we call ourselves a family. Our design team comes from all over America: modern painters, photographers and rock album designers create book covers we're proud to be judged by.

We publish and promote 8-12 tour-savvy authors per year. We are grass-roots, D.I.Y., bootstrap believers. Pull up a good book and join the family. Support independent authors, artists and presses.

**Want to know more about Write Bloody books, authors, and events?
Join our mailing list at**

www.writebloody.com

WRITE BLOODY BOOKS

CPSIA information can be obtained at www.ICGtesting.com
Printed in the USA
BVOW02s1649161013

333851BV00008B/10/P